"Don't use guilt on me, Cole. I don't appreciate it. I'll spend as much spare time as I can with Madeline, but you have to find someone who can care for the children full-time. Okay?"

Cole nodded, but she wasn't at all certain she'd gotten through to him.

"I mean it, Cole. I expect you to put in your best effort to find someone else."

"I will," he promised, and she believed him.

A tiny head peered around Cole's legs: Madeline, her blue eyes a miniature version of her uncle's, but large in her tiny face. Every bit as haunted as his, they softened Honey's defenses, and that would not do.

She couldn't offer everything Cole needed, but she would give as much as she could.

Dear Reader,

Since writing the first book in my Rodeo, Montana series I have wanted to write Cole Payette and Honey Armstrong's story!

I liked both of these characters immensely and included them in the other books in the series. Cole is a capable, intelligent, well-respected sheriff, but he falls apart whenever Honey is around. Usually articulate, Cole is extremely shy with her and can't string two words together when she is near. Honey owns the town's bar and is outgoing and generous.

When Cole becomes guardian of two sad children, and is grief-stricken himself at the loss of his sister, the first person he goes to is Honey. With the help of the children, Cole learns to step outside his fears and embrace life before it slips through his fingers. Watching Honey fall in love with the already-smitten Cole was a lot of fun. Together, the duo provides the children with a new and loving home.

I hope you enjoy reading this story as much as I enjoyed writing it!

Mary Sullivan

RODEO SHERIFF

Mary Sullivan

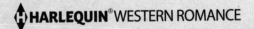
HARLEQUIN® WESTERN ROMANCE

Recycling programs
for this product may
not exist in your area.

ISBN-13: 978-1-335-69956-5

Rodeo Sheriff

Printed in U.S.A.

HARLEQUIN®

™ www.Harlequin.com

Author **Mary Sullivan** has been collecting awards, accolades and great reviews since her first book, *No Ordinary Cowboy*, was published by Harlequin in 2009. She has written fifteen Harlequin Superromances and four Harlequin Western Romances. She has been told her writing touches the heart.

She loves hearing from readers! To keep up-to-date about upcoming releases, don't forget to sign up for her newsletter at marysullivanbooks.com.

Books by Mary Sullivan

Harlequin Western Romance

Rodeo Father
Rodeo Rancher
Rodeo Baby

Harlequin Superromance

No Ordinary Sheriff
In from the Cold
Home to Laura
Because of Audrey
Always Emily
No Ordinary Home
Safe in Noah's Arms
Cody's Come Home

Visit the Author Profile page
at Harlequin.com for more titles.

Chapter One

Honey Armstrong wouldn't have thought Rodeo's sheriff, being the predictable sort, could do much to surprise her.

Except show up with children.

Cole Payette, in civilian clothes instead of his uniform, stood just inside the open doorway of Honey's empty bar with two kids.

The cloudless June day cast Cole and the children into silhouette.

Sunlight limned Cole's muscular frame and lightened his thatch of dirty-blond hair.

His broad shoulders dwarfed the silent, delicate girl about three or four years old sitting on his forearm. A boy of about six held Cole's other hand, but not quietly. His slim body percolated in motion.

Honey's spirits lifted, and she laughed. "I was just thinking I need a distraction this afternoon."

For Honey, a child was a luminous slice of life, the perfect soft golden yolk of a sunny-side-up egg.

Cole wasn't a father, nor did he babysit that she knew of, even though the children of town liked him.

So whose kids were they?

"Who do you have with you today, Cole?"

He sighed and Honey cocked her head, alerted by a strange intensity emanating from him.

While Cole might have lived in town for more than a dozen years, his presence on his favorite bar stool at Honey's Place every Friday and Saturday night accounted for most of Honey's exposure to him. He poured drinks while she took her breaks or relieved her waiters. Cole didn't visit any other time unless on official business.

So why was he here with children on Sunday when he knew the bar was closed? Had something happened to someone in town?

"Come in," she urged again. "Close the door." Eager to recognize the children, she gestured for them to step closer. "Who did you bring to visit?"

"They're mine," Cole said, his voice a hollowed-out shell of its normal deep timbre.

Honey frowned.

Mine?

As owner of the only bar in town, Honey knew all that went on in Rodeo. Cole had no children and no significant other. Unless maybe he lived a double life he kept secret… Ha. In Rodeo? Where everyone knew everything about everyone? Laughable.

"Shut the door," she said, quietly this time. She knew trouble when it walked into her bar.

He did so, blocking out the sunshine. He stepped closer to the lamps, a ravaged man who looked as though he'd been on a bender last night. If so, it hadn't been here. He'd been missing from town all week, his bar stool empty last night and Friday night.

Deep brackets framed his well-defined mouth, harsher than usual.

Honey was certain he wasn't yet thirty-five, but permanent frown lines had already started to develop on his forehead, and today every faint line that marred his attractive face was deeper than usual.

He watched her with a dim, weary gaze, as did the boy and girl, all three seeming past their power to endure.

The boy shifted from foot to foot.

"Do you need to go to the bathroom?" Honey asked the child.

"Nope," he said loudly.

Cole stared down at him. "He moves a lot."

Okay. But— *They're mine?*

"What do you mean, they're yours?" Honey asked.

"They were my sister's kids."

Honey gasped. *Were.*

Grief rolled from Cole in dark waves.

After staring at Honey with wide eyes for unrelieved moments, the girl closed her eyes, rested her head on Cole's shoulder and stuck her tiny thumb into her mouth.

Honey's heart went out to her.

Help, Cole mouthed. One word. So much said.

She started to rush forward, but he stiffened, resisting her sympathy.

Okay. As always with Cole, she got mixed messages. He would help her out at the bar on the weekends, but outside of that, hands off.

You got it, Cole. Message received.

And yet here he was in her empty bar with a pair of children.

Okay. Today he needed her, but no physical displays of sympathy. Maybe he was too close to the edge. Given her experience with her mother's and Daniel's deaths, she understood.

"What can I do?" she asked briskly.

"The kids will need someone to take care of them. I have to get organized. I— Maybe I have to get them... I don't know. What? A nanny?"

Ordinarily, Cole would know that kind of thing, but

shock had a firm hold on him. "A nanny, yes," she confirmed. "What do you need from me?"

"Can you take care of the children while I interview people?"

"Today? Now? That's so soon. You just brought them to town."

He didn't respond, but his hard jaw flexed.

Honey went on, "Can you take time off work to get them settled in? If you give them over to a nanny too soon, won't that be hard on them?"

He shrugged helplessly, this normally rock-solid guy. "I'm taking this week off, but I need to get as much as possible settled right away."

Maybe a gradual transition was a good idea, kind of acclimating the children to the new nanny before Cole left them with her full-time.

"Okay."

"I don't know what I'm doing. I'm in over my head." A massive admission from a man most often in control. "I can't do this alone."

"I'll help, of course, but I don't understand. Why come to the bar? Why come to me?"

"You're good with kids," he said. "You love them and they love you."

Yes, true. She was crazy about kids. No secret there. Everyone in the surrounding Montana countryside knew that. Children gathered around wherever Honey went, drawn like bees to…well, honey.

"Can I do the interviews here?" he asked.

"Cole, this is a bar. I know I'm closed today and tomorrow, but still. It's hardly an appropriate spot."

Cole released the boy's hand. A couple of backpacks fell from his shoulder to the floor. Given half a chance, maybe he would follow suit.

"There's room here for me to ask questions without anyone hearing."

Anyone. The children.

"You know my place," he said. "It's dim and dismal."

"Actually, I don't." She'd never been in the apartment above the sheriff's office. "But I'll take your word for it."

She glanced around her bar. "While it's spacious, I would hardly say this is a suitable spot for entertaining children."

He stared around, but Honey had the sense he wasn't seeing much. *Oh, my lord, he looks so lost.*

Right. Let's get on with it.

"Upstairs." Brisk in her movements, she locked the front door of the bar. "We'll use my apartment."

He nodded. "Makes sense. Yeah. Thanks."

Cole Payette, as predictable as a finely wound clock, as handsome and rugged as the Rocky Mountains—and as quiet as a monk when in her presence—had reached the end of his rope.

No problem. Honey had enough coping skills for both of them.

"Follow me," she said.

She led them to the interior stairs at the back of the building.

A sudden tug on a huge hank of her hair had her pulling up short.

"Ow!"

"I'm sorry!" Cole sounded distressed.

Someone hung onto her hair with a strong grip. Honey turned around as far as she could. It was the girl in Cole's arms. He was trying to loosen her grip, but the child wouldn't let go.

Cole stared at the child in his arms. "Madeline, let go."

The child's deep, hollow gaze broke Honey's heart.

"What's going on?" she asked Cole.

"Her mother had long blond hair. I guess... I don't know... Maybe she sees a bit of her mother in you?"

Tentatively, Honey held out her hands. The child practically jumped into her arms, where she clung like a monkey.

She drew hanks of Honey's waist-length, curly hair around her shoulders as though donning a protective cape.

Honey's heart broke a little more. She raised her eyebrows at Cole, but he shook his head, also confused by the girl's behavior.

If this was what she needed, this was what Honey would give. She carried the child up to her apartment, leading Cole and the boy down the hallway to her living room.

Honey liked big comfy furniture—big comfy everything—and her space reflected that, with plenty of generous pieces for seating and lots of colorful afghans thrown around. The apartment as large as the bar below, Honey had all kinds of living space.

While Cole conducted his interviews in privacy by the windows, Honey could play with the children at the opposite end of the room.

Cole led the boy to the sofa, where he sat obediently and hugged one of her puffy pillows. When Honey tried to put down the girl, she clung hard, her tiny fingernails digging into Honey's shoulders.

Honey straightened. The girl wrapped Honey's hair more tightly about herself. Okay, this could be a problem.

She indicated the girl and boy. "Is this why you've been missing from town the past week?"

Cole nodded.

"No one knew where you went."

"Didn't tell them." His voice rasped as drily as day-old bread without a trace of butter.

The children made not a peep. The girl still had her thumb in her mouth, even though she was too old for it.

The boy played an imaginary game walking his fingers along the seams of the pillow on his lap.

This was silly. She couldn't keep calling them the boy and the girl.

"What are their names?"

"I'm Evan Engel," the boy piped up.

"Evan, I'm Honey."

"Like the stuff you put on toast?"

She smiled. "Exactly like that."

The girl didn't make a sound.

"That's Madeline," Cole said. Oh, yes, he'd used the girl's name when she'd grabbed Honey's hair.

Honey placed a hand on Cole's arm. Tension ran along his muscles.

His body reacted when she touched him with not quite a jerk, but more like— Well, she didn't know.

She dropped her hand and motioned him toward the far end of the room, to her small home office set up with desk, chair, her computer and a printer.

She ran Honey's Place from her office downstairs, but she'd designed this corner up here strictly for pleasure. Well…to be honest…to play her computer games.

Voice pitched low, she asked, "What happened to their parents?"

Stark vulnerability clouded his handsome face. His gaze flickered to Madeline.

"My sister— Her husband—" His voice broke. He hissed in a breath. "In their will, they left guardianship of the children to me."

Before she could ask for more, he rushed on, "Can we leave it at that for now?" A pain-laden plea if she'd ever heard one.

She'd always wanted a sister.

"Was she your only sibling?" she asked.

He tightened his lips and nodded.

God. To have only one sister and to lose her so early in life, and then to have an instant family. How was he to deal with this?

And Evan and Madeline, poor children.

No! She would not use that awful, inadequate, destructive word *poor*.

From personal experience, starting with her father's death when she was only six, she knew too well the damage a word like that could do to a child…and how dangerous pity was. She would not treat Madeline or Evan with that most useless of emotions, pity.

They should never think of themselves as *poor*.

How could she help them?

Perhaps by making the day as normal as possible.

"Before you use the phone to set up your interviews, I need to call Rachel to come over."

"Go ahead and use your phone," Cole said. "I'll use my cell. Why Rachel?"

"We need to make the children comfortable. Rachel will bring Tori. If anyone can put them at ease it's that little girl."

The tension in Cole's shoulders eased a fraction. "Yeah. Good idea." He stretched his neck to one side and then to the other. Bones popped. "Who should I call in town?"

"To hire as a nanny?"

He nodded.

Honey tapped her lips with her forefinger. "Of the women who would suit, there are Ellen Clarkson, Tanya Mayhall and Maria Tripoli."

"All older women. Why?"

"They've been stay-at-home moms, and their chicks have flown the nest. They're helping to organize the teenagers for the food and beverage stands at the revival fair. They love children and are good with them."

Cole nodded and collapsed into her office chair. "Sounds good."

He pulled his cell phone out of his shirt pocket and stared at it as if it were alien to him.

Honey touched his hand, surprising him. He glanced up with wide blue eyes. Something odd touched their depths. Maybe hope? Or...what? Honey couldn't identify what she saw, but again tension arced under her fingers.

She dropped her hand. "Do you need me to make the calls?"

A split second of temptation lit the darkness in his eyes, replaced at once by determination.

"My job. Just please take care of them this afternoon. Make them happy."

"Cole, no one can do that right now."

"You can, Honey. If anyone can, it's you."

Tightening her hold on Madeline, she huffed out a frustrated sigh. What a burden he was placing on her. She might be a favorite with the children of Rodeo, Montana, but she wasn't a miracle worker.

His intensity, while understandable given the situation, unnerved her. He wasn't thinking rationally.

"Oh, Cole." Her voice eased out of her on a breath of soft air. "It's too early. There's nothing that will make them *happy*. All I can do is make them comfortable."

"Do that? Please?" The rawness in his voice held her still.

How could she resist a plea so sweetly asked?

"Okay. You make the calls and get those women in here to interview. I'll take care of the children."

She squeezed his hand, meaning to move on quickly, but he turned his palm up and grasped her like he never meant to let go. His grip became painful.

He closed his eyes. Misery etched deeper those brackets of character on his face.

When he looked at her again, moisture shimmered on his pale lashes.

Tenderness welled inside Honey.

She did affection *really* well, especially with children and friends, but affection toward men? Not so much. She had her reasons, all balled up in an amalgam of passionate love and too much loss…as well as being a female bar owner.

She straightened and put distance between herself and that dangerous tenderness.

He dropped her hand.

All business, she offered, "Would you like coffee? Food?"

He shook his head. "I don't want to put you out."

Used to dealing with recalcitrant drunks, she slammed her fist onto her unoccupied hip. "When did you last eat?"

He turned inward but couldn't seem to come up with an answer. "I don't remember."

"And the children?"

"Breakfast this morning."

"It's two o'clock. I'll put on the coffeepot and get food in here." She pointed a finger at his face. "When the children sit down to eat, so will you."

She snagged the phone and walked to her bedroom at the back of the apartment, hitching Madeline a little higher on her hip.

Rachel answered on the second ring. "Hi, Honey. What's up?"

"Are you and the children available this afternoon?"

"Sure. Travis is out checking on the herd. What do you need?"

"Come over."

"Now? Beth is napping."

Aware of Madeline listening in, Honey said, "Can you come anyway? Right away? There are a couple of children here who need someone to play with. They need Tori. I'll explain when you arrive."

Despite how little Honey was actually telling her, Rachel responded with an immediate, "Okay, we'll be right over. I'll have to wake Beth, so she might be grumpy."

Honey considered baby Beth's discomfort a small price to pay for providing Evan and Madeline with small-fry company.

"See you soon."

Next, Honey called Violet Summer, who owned the Summertime Diner.

After a few rings, Vy answered. "Hey, Honey. To what do I owe the annoyance of this call interrupting a perfectly fine Sunday afternoon with my man?"

Honey laughed. God, she loved Vy's irreverent sense of humor. On the other hand, Vy might be serious considering how recently her relationship with newcomer Sam Carmichael had begun.

Honey explained that she had children and a couple of adults who needed to be fed, and that it was an emergency. She could almost feel Vy coming alert like a bird dog sensing prey.

"I'll head over to the diner and see what Will has left over from yesterday. It might not be much. We were busy. I'll get there as soon as I can."

Once Vy arrived with food, Honey would assess what was needed and call in her cook, Chet, to make up burgers and fries if necessary. Honey didn't have enough food in the apartment for everyone. She didn't think Madeline would let go of her long enough for Honey to buy food, let alone cook it. A good guy who liked children, Chet wouldn't mind cooking for them.

Honey had forgotten to ask Cole whether she could share his story, but it would be naive of him to think he could hold on to this forever. The second he'd brought the children home with him to Rodeo, they'd become part of the community.

Hold up, Honey. You don't even know if this is permanent. But Cole mentioned guardianship and a will, so probably?

She would just have to get the full story at some point.

Back in the living room, she replaced the phone in its cradle. Cole sat staring at his cell, but at least there'd been some progress. He'd made a list of the women with their contact information.

Honey picked up the sheet of paper. "You know their phone numbers?"

Cole's eyebrows shot up. "I contacted the office. The deputy on duty accessed the town's database."

"Oh. Of course." She pointed to Tanya's name and said, "Call her first. Tell her to be here in an hour if she can."

"Not right away?"

"No. You're going to eat first."

She tried to put Madeline down on the sofa again, but the little girl still clung.

Honey hitched her a bit higher. Good thing she was strong from running her bar and hauling around cases of liquor and beer.

One-handed, she put on a pot of coffee to brew and got out mugs, cream and sugar.

She poured a cup of coffee for Cole and brought it to him.

"You look numb," she said.

Cole stared at her.

Frowning, she returned to the kitchen to pour a mug for herself.

The front doorbell tinkled. Company. Honey ran down the stairs to let in Rachel, Beth and Tori.

Thank God. The cavalry had arrived.

Four-year-old Tori threw herself against Honey's legs.

"Mommy said you gots kids here. Who's that girl you're holding? Can I meet her?"

"You sure can." *This*, Tori's boundless excitement, was exactly what these two waifs needed, but Madeline burrowed into Honey's hair. "You can meet her upstairs."

In the living room, Tori ran to the sofa and stared at Evan. "I'm Tori. I live in Rodeo. Who are you?"

"I'm Evan. That's my sister, Madeline."

"I like your names." She pointed to the sofa. "Can I sit here?"

From behind the curtain of Honey's hair, Madeline studied Tori, not emitting a sound.

Tori wasn't bossy by nature, but she was friendly and exuberant. As far as Honey could tell, she had decided to take control.

"You look nice," she said to Madeline. "Sit here." She curled up beside Evan and patted the sofa beside herself.

Madeline merely stared.

"We be friends," Tori said. "I brought games. We can play."

The tiniest of smiles hovered on Evan's lips. Madeline rested her head on Honey's shoulder and stayed where she was.

Tori frowned, not used to resistance.

Honey frowned, too. If Tori couldn't break through Madeline's shell, who could?

Chapter Two

Numb.

Honey thought Cole was numb.

If only.

Cole wished to hell he was truly numb all the way through to his core. He wished he never had to feel another emotion in his life again. Then he wouldn't have to be this raw, pain-ravaged creature.

This aching, furious, grief-stricken man with every nerve exposed and crawling.

His reactions might be slow, but numb? No.

Sandy. His baby sister was gone. Her bright-burning presence would no longer illuminate this world. A shining star of a woman had been snuffed out too early.

He couldn't wrap his head it. He couldn't accept that he would never see her again.

Never.

Dennis Engle, her husband, had been a good guy. Cole had liked and respected the man. Gone too young, too.

Cole's parents were still alive, but he hoped never to see them again in his lifetime.

His family had been reduced to those two orphans on the sofa.

He wasn't up to this. He'd faced every challenge life had ever thrown at him and had survived. But this?

God.

How—?

God.

There were no words.

Numb?

A bitter laugh burst out of him. If freaking only.

No anesthetic in this world could kill his pain.

He dredged up every trace of strength he had left inside his hollowed-out shell of a soul.

As sheriff, he knew everyone in town. Tanya was good people. He phoned her. She answered on the third ring.

He told her why he was calling. "You wouldn't start for at least a week, but I need—I need—"

"To get things settled and planned," she said. "I understand. I'll see you in an hour, Cole."

He ended the call.

What now?

What was he supposed to ask her and the other women?

Studying the children, he tried to imagine what they would need on a day-to-day basis while he was at work.

Discipline? Strong, but loving.

Education? Age appropriate and not overwhelming.

Fun? God, yes.

Affection? Hell, yeah. Plenty of it. As much as their little hearts could hold.

He wanted things settled. Now.

Despite the sun streaming through Honey's windows, he shivered.

He'd never felt so alone.

How was he supposed to raise those children on his own?

HONEY LED HER friend to her bedroom, where Rachel took off Beth's tiny sweater and hat.

"Spill," Rachel ordered. "What's going on?"

Honey patted Madeline's back. "Evan and Madeline are Cole's nephew and niece." She glanced at Madeline, who continued to hide behind Honey's hair. "Isn't that nice?"

Rachel must have caught Honey's warning look that said *we'll talk later*, because she murmured, "I see."

"Cole is interviewing caregivers for the children today. If Tanya Mayhall agreed, she should be here soon."

Rachel stared at Madeline with a worried frown and pointed discreetly. Honey glanced down. A wide frill decorated the neckline of Honey's white blouse. Madeline had a small piece of it in her mouth, sucking on it. "Oh... I—"

Honey covered her lips with her fingers and fought tears.

"It will be okay," Rachel said, too loudly. "Tanya's a great woman. She loves children."

"Yes." Honey cleared a sudden huskiness out of her throat.

Rachel nodded toward the child, whose hands still grasped bunches of Honey's hair.

"She likes being held by you."

Honey nodded and gave a rundown on the other two women she'd also suggested.

"All perfect candidates. I would trust my children with any of them."

"I hope he can do a good job of interviewing," Honey said. "Cole's even worse than usual because of this."

Puzzled, Rachel asked, "Worse than usual? How so?"

"You know Cole. So quiet."

"Quiet? What do you mean?"

"He's like one of those monks who makes a vow of silence."

Rachel frowned and lifted Beth into her arms. "I've never noticed that. He chats away whenever we meet, always asking about the children and curious about how Travis's herd is doing."

"Um, is he like that with Travis, too?"

"They've become great friends. He's like that with everyone. Haven't you ever seen him in the diner when he goes in for breakfast?"

"With the hours I keep at the bar, I usually sleep through Vy's breakfast hours."

"Oh, right, of course. Anyway, he does the rounds before sitting down to have breakfast."

Curious. Cole had always been quiet with her, and she didn't know why.

He might share a conversation with someone on a bar stool beside him, but he certainly didn't talk to *her*. She'd assumed it was because she was so busy and he didn't want to intrude. Looked like she was wrong.

Come on, Honey, you've seen him chatting with the townspeople. You knew he avoided you outside the bar.

She'd kind of ignored that.

It hurt that Cole wasn't friendly with her—only a little, but even so. What on earth did Cole have against Honey that he was talkative with the rest of the town, but not with her?

Then he shows up here today with children, trusting me to take care of them. Cole, who the heck are you?

"Come on," Rachel said, leaving the bedroom. "Let's go see what we can do for him."

When they returned to the living room, Rachel put Beth down on the short end of the L-shaped sofa and surrounded her with pillows.

She approached Cole, who accepted a long hug.

Honey watched him wrap his strong arms around her friend and close his eyes, dipping his chin onto Rachel's hair.

Downstairs in the bar, he'd stepped away from Honey's attempt at sympathy.

Tori spoke up, breaking into her thoughts. "Can we

build a fort, Honey?" She pointed to Madeline. "Would she like it?"

Honey's eyebrows shot up. "I don't know. We could build one and see?"

Tori smiled. "'Kay."

Honey kissed Tori's cheek. "Love you, sweetheart."

"I love you, too, Honey, but we needs to build our fort now."

Madeline peeked between strands of Honey's hair and watched the interchange between Tori and Honey with a frown furrowing her small brow.

COLE PAYETTE LOVED Honey Armstrong.

He couldn't remember a time when he hadn't.

He'd been careful to never show his feelings to her. Years ago, he'd made big mistakes with a woman. Deep in his soul, he knew that wasn't a path he could take again. It was even more important now that he had the responsibility of raising two children.

No matter how great she was with kids, Honey was too much a free spirit for him.

She might be good at making children laugh, but those kids were going to need a firmly measured guiding hand.

Honey, pretty and generous and fun, was so achingly attractive to Cole that he had trouble not giving in to his need for her. He'd resisted her allure for years while she ran her bar—a bar, for God's sake—made friends with all of her customers, and kept unconventional hours.

Her business was important to Honey. He suspected it was everything for her. How could she possibly have a family? How could she spend her evenings running a bar, go to bed at two in the morning and then be there for her children the next day? It would never happen.

It could never work.

But look at how she held Madeline and rested her chin on the girl's head while she smiled and kissed Tori.

Honey messed with Cole's head, and had done so for at least a decade.

He heard her murmur, "I have to put you down to make a fort."

Madeline turned her face into Honey's chest.

Honey shot him a look that said, *Help*.

He stood and took Madeline from her.

Honey rushed around the apartment gathering afghans and blankets, tearing her place apart to make an indoor playground for the children.

She pushed two armchairs together and threw a couple of afghans over their high backs. A third armchair joined the first two, leaving the side facing the windows open. She tucked cushions inside.

She disappeared down the back hallway. Cole heard her running down the stairs.

Across the room, Rachel smiled at him. "Whirlwind," she said.

He nodded.

A minute later Honey returned, carrying a pair of microphone stands. She collapsed them to their shortest heights and hooked the corners of each afghan onto them, effectively creating a cozy, private nook for the children.

"Yay!" Evan jumped up from the sofa and ran into the fort. "Madeline, come on. This is great!"

Only once her brother had invited her in did Madeline climb down from Cole's arms and sit in an armchair in the cozy alcove.

Tori sat in the last empty chair and spread her hands. "Do you like it? Honey makes good forts."

Subdued, Madeline sat still and self-contained, while Evan punched pillows into comfortable shapes. Tori's chatter cracked their shells. Infinitesimal fissures, but there nonetheless.

Good instinct on Honey's part to get Tori here.

Madeline still sucked her thumb. Evan beat an edgy tattoo with his heels against the armchair.

They're mine.

God above, how was Cole to cope?

Before he fell into that trap of despair again, he called the last two women and set up their appointments an hour apart. Best to get this all over with today for his own peace of mind.

Tori peeked around the corner of an afghan and asked, "Honey, can we have snacks?"

"In a few minutes. Vy's bringing food from the diner."

"Vy's coming over!" Tori clapped her hands. "Is Chels coming, too?"

The town had welcomed Sam Carmichael and his daughter, Chelsea, just a couple of months ago, and already they were fast friends with the entire group of women revitalizing the town fair. For over a hundred years, it had drawn people from miles around for a full week every August, but it had closed down fifteen years ago when the owner had grown too old to keep up with the work.

Now, six local women, including Honey, were reviving it and restoring the rides for a new run for a week in August, hoping to bring in tourists and locals alike, and much needed income for the town.

Honey was in charge of refreshment stands and had already ordered the supplies and hired local women and students to prepare the food and run the booths.

As sheriff, Cole made a point of keeping up-to-date on everything going on in town, particularly the arrival of strangers.

After a rocky start, Sam had turned out to be the fair owner's grandson and an okay guy, even pairing up with the town's diner owner. An unlikely friendship had developed between newly adolescent Chelsea and four-year-old Tori.

"Is Chels coming?" Tori repeated.

"I think only Vy," Honey said.

Tori scrambled out of the armchair. "Mommy, I needs your phone. I gots to call Vy. She needs to bring Chels."

Rachel handed her cell to her daughter. Like a miniature expert, the child unlocked it, located the number and placed the call.

"It's Tori, Vy! Hi! Bring Chels to Honey's house, okay?"

Silence while Tori listened, followed by an argument. "She will so want to come. Please? My friend Mad and me needs hot-pink nail polish with sparkles. Ask her, okay?"

Again silence and then Tori said, "Okay. See you soon. Love you!" A second later, she squealed, "Love you, three!" and disconnected. She returned to the armchair fort, throwing back over her shoulder, "Chels is coming."

Cole smiled. That child could move mountains.

A moment later, Tori backed out of the fort. From Cole's spot at the sunny end of the room, he noted her distress.

"Mommy, Mad is crying." Tori looked just this side of giving in to tears herself.

Cole moved to intervene, but Rachel got there first and placed a comforting hand on her daughter's shoulder.

"What's wrong?" Rachel asked.

Madeline crooked one tiny finger at Tori, who leaned close and listened to the whispering in her ear. "She said she's not Mad."

"Of course she isn't. Why did you call her mad?"

"Her name is long. I gives everybody a nickname, Mommy."

"Fair enough. 'Madeline' is a mouthful. She might like Maddy. It's pretty. Try it out and see what her reaction is."

Tori leaned close to Madeline. "Your name is long. I can call you Maddy, okay?"

Madeline nodded, and peace was restored.

Rachel reached to wipe Madeline's cheeks, but she reared back. Honey exchanged a glance with her friend.

Since the funeral, only Cole had been able to hold Madeline. She wouldn't even go to his sister's best friend. But she'd wanted Honey to hold her.

He'd thought maybe Madeline was softening. But she'd rejected Rachel, who was about as warm as a person could be, who loved children, and who was loved by children in return.

How was Madeline going to be with Tanya? Cole hadn't expected this wrinkle.

His legs wanted to pace. His feet itched to carry him far away.

A breath whooshed out of him. He'd pushed through the past week with sheer discipline, but now that he was home in Rodeo, he'd hit a wall.

And yet, he had so far to go. His new life had only just begun, with no time for fatigue. In coming home, he hadn't reached the end, but a beginning.

He didn't have a clue how to live this new life.

He scrubbed a hand over his face, his palm rasping across his unshaven jaw.

He drained the last of his coffee. Honey was right. The warm drink had restored a semblance of calm.

Needing another one, he stood. Already way ahead of him, Honey took his mug and refilled it.

He had to resist her allure.

If he let himself go, he would grab hold of her and never, ever release her again.

He wanted Honey that badly.

Her touch staggered him, weakened him and made him wish for things he knew could never be.

That bit of foolishness when he'd taken her hand and held on for dear life had been a mistake, simply his neediness taking over.

He loved her.

He shouldn't. He knew in his heart they wouldn't suit each other. Experience had taught him irreversible lessons.

Case closed.

She handed his coffee then stepped away, passing through a shaft of sunlight. His breath caught.

She really was one of the prettiest women for miles around. Honey's deep-set blue eyes studied the world with captivating intelligence. Long, blond curls touched the base of her spine. A wide-necked white blouse fell from one shoulder while a belt cinched in her waist above a flowing blue skirt. Turquoise and silver jewelry at wrists, ears and throat shone in the sunbeam.

Her lush figure, pocket-size compared to his six-one frame, well... Cole swallowed. He couldn't dwell on that too much. He'd ached for her for too long.

Best to ignore physical desires.

The absolute perfection of Honey Armstrong, though, was her smile—the one she flashed often for every man, woman and child in Rodeo. It turned prettiness into beauty.

Cole turned away and steeled himself.

The door that separated the apartment from the stairs down to the street opened. Violet Summer burst into the room. Exactly the kind of entrance bold, confident Vy liked to make. She waved to Cole at the other end of the living room. He raised one hand in a modified version of Vy's flamboyance.

He liked Vy a lot. She was one of the town's go-to sources of good common sense in the midst of any crisis. Plus, she sold great food at respectable prices and treated everyone with sincere, if sarcastic, good humor.

Chelsea followed her in, and Tori launched herself at her friend. They hugged.

"Did you bringed the nail polish?" Tori asked.

"What do you think, pipsqueak?"

Tori giggled. "'Kay."

They put boxes on the counter that separated the kitchen from the living room and unloaded them. They must have cleaned out *all* of the diner's Saturday leftovers.

Honey took Vy's hand and led her down the hallway. Rachel followed. Cole knew what that meant—his story being shared.

He hated it, loathed this laying bare of his life, but he expected it. The whole town would, and should, know of it soon enough.

Rodeo was now the home of his sister's two children, and the townspeople needed to get to know them.

He knew everything there was to know about his fellow citizens. Why shouldn't they know about him? He'd protected his past from them, though. That was his and his alone.

But the children's story would spread, naturally.

Vy strode back into the living room and made a bee-line for him. He stood to catch her in his arms when she grasped him to her curvy body.

She held on for long moments, whispering, "I'm sorry."

They both knew it was inadequate, but her concern was welcome nonetheless.

When he could take no more of her sympathy, he set her away from him. He glanced down and smiled to relieve the grief building in him like a pressure cooker about to blow.

God knew he didn't want to cry in front of these women and the children. That would set off everyone, especially Evan and Madeline.

"Is it my imagination, or are you showing?"

Vy swatted his shoulder. "A man should never discuss

a woman's weight." She dropped the fake outrage and grinned. "Yeah, I'm finally showing. Isn't it awesome?"

If his answering grin wobbled around the edges, it was to be expected. He was happy for Vy, and Sam Carmichael, too, and glad they'd found each other even if the pregnancy had come shockingly quickly. Cole had no right to envy.

Vy deserved all of this and more.

When Vy turned to walk away, Cole noticed Honey watching with a frown.

What was that about?

Vy stooped in front of little Madeline.

"Hi," she said and held out her hand.

Madeline didn't take it.

Vy turned and tickled Tori until she giggled with delight. Tori and Vy were great friends.

Madeline and Evan watched with fascination, as well they might. Cole hadn't been able to give them a damned bit of pleasure this past week.

He wished he knew more about their lives with his sister and her husband. His twice-yearly visits hadn't been nearly enough to forge as strong a bond as he'd have liked with his nephew and niece.

He needed one now, this minute, but God knew how long that would take with the children so damaged.

He watched Honey placing bowls on place mats. Then she called the children to come and sit at the table.

When Madeline sat down, she started to cry.

Cole rushed over and picked her up. She cuddled her head against his chest. He knew she liked the vibrations his voice made when he talked. "What's wrong?"

"Raisins," she whispered for his ears only.

Honey had given the children Vy's amazing rice pudding, some of the best comfort food on earth, thick with custard and sprinkled with nutmeg, but Madeline was obviously offended by the raisins.

"She doesn't like raisins. Is there something else she can have?" He picked up her bowl to put it in the kitchen, but Tori's high-pitched voice stopped him.

"Sheriff, no! I gots a *big* love for raisins. I eat them."

A big love. Good lord, Tori was cute. No wonder she broke down resistance wherever she went.

He set the bowl back on the table.

"Maddy, do you likes rice pudding without raisins?" Tori asked.

Madeline nodded.

"I eat your raisins and you eat the pudding. Okay?"

Madeline nodded.

"Mommy, can you putted the raisins from Maddy's pudding in my bowl?"

"I'll do it," Cole said. Tori might be here for the children's sake, but her open, honest spirit soothed Cole as well. When he finished, the children ate.

Honey approached and rested her fingers on his arm to get his attention. He sidled away. He might crave contact with her, but Honey touching him constituted a dangerous, subversive act against his vulnerable defenses.

She was not the woman for him, he reminded himself yet again.

"Here," she said, handing him a plate of reheated meat loaf and mashed potatoes. He could smell the garlic in them. The Summertime Diner's food was the best.

"Eat," Honey ordered.

He sat down in the remaining empty chair not at all certain he could swallow a bite. But he tried.

Minutes later, he'd finished the entire plate.

"Better?" Vy asked.

He nodded. A second later, Honey appeared at his side with a bowl of rice pudding for him, too, her floral essence swirling around her.

Madeline grasped a hank of Honey's hair and held on,

forcing Honey to pick her up, sit down in her chair and put the child on her lap.

Madeline pulled Honey's hair around her head and under her chin like a nun's wimple, leaving only a narrow portion of her face showing.

Cole put down his spoon and squeezed the bridge of his nose. How was he supposed to make life normal for children who had lost so much?

Honey picked up a bit of Maddy's rice pudding in a spoon and fed it to her. Maddy let her.

Cole had been having trouble getting enough food into the child. Thank God for Honey.

The apartment door opened and Will, Vy's cook, stepped in carrying a tray.

Cole glanced at Vy.

She grinned. "I asked him to make milk shakes and bring them over."

Cole frowned. "On a Sunday? You shouldn't have. It's his day off."

"I don't mind," Will said. "Nothing much else to do."

That surprised Cole. Will was a big handsome guy with a wicked set of dimples that set the women of Rodeo sighing. No exaggeration. Cole had witnessed the weird phenomenon of usually sensible women falling all over Will when he indulged them with one of his rare smiles.

The women of town pursued. Will resisted. Cole had no idea why.

With a magician's flourish, Will snatched the towel from the tray to reveal a half dozen small milk shakes in retro diner glasses.

"Who wants one?"

All three tiny heads nodded, as did Chelsea.

"Who are these two little ones I haven't met?"

"I'm Evan."

Will shook his hand.

Madeline didn't say a word. "That's my sister, Madeline," Evan clarified.

Will leaned close. Madeline stared at the colorful drinks. "I have vanilla, chocolate and strawberry. What is your choice?"

Will made no mention of the odd way Maddy sat surrounded by Honey's hair. Good man.

Madeline pointed to a pink milk shake. Will put it on the place mat in front of her, then asked Evan, Tori and Chelsea which flavors they preferred.

The front doorbell rang.

"It's like Grand Central Station in here," Cole muttered before remembering he was interviewing today.

God, he was tired.

Honey headed downstairs. The room had filled up with adults and children, but the second Honey left, so did all of the room's warmth.

Cole's mantra—*if Honey is there, I am aware*—ran through him.

She returned with Tanya Mayhall.

Tanya, a solidly built, affectionate middle-aged woman with not one sharp edge about her, searched the room for Cole with a worried frown.

He stood and approached.

As naturally as the sun rose each day, she took him into her arms.

He went willingly.

If ever a woman was designed to be a mother, it was Tanya. Madeline and Evan might need mothering right now, but, strangely, so did Cole.

Tanya had a strong grip. He returned it. She enveloped him with not only the warmth of her affection and empathy but also a complex cloud of lavender and vanilla.

Cole sighed.

"I'm sorry, my dear," Tanya whispered. Her response

did nothing to change what had happened but was heart-felt and welcome.

Over her shoulder, Cole again noted a puzzling frown from Honey.

Chapter Three

Honey watched another woman embrace Cole.

Why should it bother her? That flash of tenderness toward him earlier had unnerved her with its intensity. She didn't harbor hopes of a relationship with Cole. So why feel jealous because he was taking hugs from other women? For a woman who knew her own mind, this confusion didn't sit well with Honey.

Tanya released Cole but held his face between her hands and spoke quietly. The tension in Cole's shoulders eased.

Tanya brushed a hand across the creases on his brow, and Honey could almost see Cole's burden lighten.

What was Tanya saying? What words of comfort did she have for Cole that Honey hadn't managed to come up with?

She'd never felt this lack in herself before.

Why did she feel awkward with Cole, not in everyday life, but now that there was something out of the ordinary happening to him? Now that she was called on to see him differently?

To maybe not take his presence for granted?

Tanya turned to the rest of the group and said hello. A still-handsome woman in her late fifties, she'd raised four great children.

She could certainly handle these two little ones.

When Tanya stepped close to the table and talked to the children, Madeline wouldn't let Tanya touch her.

Tanya returned to the far end of the room with Cole.

Honey sent the children back into their armchair fort. Chelsea, no longer a child but not yet an adult, either, was allowed into their tiny circle.

Honey poured a cup of tea and brought it to Tanya.

Did Cole even know the right questions to ask a nanny?

He glanced at her, and, in that brief meeting of eyes, she saw doubt.

He gestured with his head for Honey to join them.

Honey knew he was capable. He interviewed criminals all the time. But this was different. Maybe he felt overwhelmed.

WHEN HONEY HANDED the cup of tea to Tanya and her arm brushed Cole's shoulder, he struggled not to pull away from her touch, from all of the good feelings she engendered in him. Feelings that scorched where his skin had thinned with grief and need.

He wanted Honey.

He had always wanted her.

He had nowhere to put these feelings, no one he could trust with them.

Honey would never trample his heart, but his judgment had been poor in the past and could be poor still, and it was all tangled up with the awful way he'd been raised.

Normally he could deal with how she affected him and could hide his feelings, but not now when his emotions were a teardrop away.

Not now when he wanted to bury himself in Honey's grace and good humor and never let go.

Silently, he asked her to join him in the interview. Maybe she would catch something he missed. Maybe she knew something children needed that he hadn't thought of.

Tanya watched it all with eyes that saw too much.

He hadn't fooled her. He didn't think the town knew how he felt about Honey, but Tanya had just caught a glimpse, and that left him uncomfortable. It angered him.

Unacceptable.

Maybe that was why his questions became tougher than merely determining her hours of availability and how she felt about children.

"How would you spend your time with Evan and Madeline?"

"They're young still. It's already June so school is over for the year, but I would teach them every day. Along with playtime, they would have studies."

"Studies?" At Madeline's age? In the cave, with the barest touch, Chelsea applied hot-pink polish to Madeline's tiny fingernails.

Madeline watched Chelsea intently. There was barely anything there to paint, those little nails small and fragile.

God, anything, *everything* could hurt that child. And what about Evan? He put on a better show than Madeline, but Cole knew how much he cried at night for his parents.

"Madeline is young," he said. Petite. Vulnerable. Depending on him to protect her. "What would those studies look like?"

"It's never too early to start teaching the alphabet."

God! The alphabet! "But *how* would you do that?"

"By showing it to her every day. By reading books and teaching her simple words."

"That doesn't sound like fun," he said.

"Cole, it would be normal for a child her age," Honey said, watching him with a frown. "Children as young as two can sing the alphabet and enjoy doing so. What Tanya is offering is appropriate."

"But—" Cole couldn't articulate why it bothered him. "Tanya, what is your teaching background?"

Her eyes widened. "I don't have a teacher's certificate. You know that, Cole. I'll use the same methods I used with my four children who are all at college now. They're smart young people."

"Yes, they are." Cole knew that, but he glanced at Evan and Madeline, looking too solemn for their ages. "I just want them to have fun." A little desperately, he added, "Just for the summer."

Tanya and Honey exchanged a glance. In it, he saw worry. Was he being unreasonable? God, he didn't know.

"Tanya, thanks for coming in today." Cole stood and Tanya followed. "I have a couple of other candidates to interview. I'll call, okay?"

Tanya looked puzzled.

He'd ended the interview too abruptly. His timing and instincts were way off.

"Sure thing, Cole."

Five minutes later, after she said goodbye to everyone and tried again to connect with Madeline, who turned away, Cole escorted her out of the apartment.

When he came back upstairs, Honey asked quietly, "What was that about?"

"What do you mean?"

"Evan and Madeline are not too young to learn. Sure, Madeline won't start kindergarten in August, but there's always preschool."

Cole dug in. "Madeline's too young to go to school, even preschool."

"Are you afraid she's not ready to meet new kids? She might be by August."

Cole crossed his arms. "Maybe."

"Okay then, maybe, but Tanya's idea of reading to her often and teaching her the alphabet is strong."

"Maybe."

Honey hissed out a breath. "Cole, you are not going to

damage those children by teaching them. Tanya's ideas are a low-pressure way to prepare Madeline for school."

"School!" he spat out. "How can we talk about school? Look at how tiny she is." He pointed toward the fort. "She's only three and a half years old!"

Honey backed away from him, and he realized he was looming over her. He eased off.

Honey's shoulders relaxed. "It's not as if Tanya was suggesting drills and flash cards."

"Yeah, but…" He didn't have a good reason for not choosing Tanya.

"Cole, I know you're scared—"

"I'm not scared."

Honey crossed her arms and stared at him.

"I—" Okay, he *was* scared. All of it—the new parenting, hiring a nanny, being responsible for kids who were still crying at night because they missed their parents— terrified him. "It's a big decision."

Honey softened. "Yes, it is."

"They cry at night," he admitted and her expression softened.

"I understand."

Cole shrugged. "I— Honey, I don't know why, but Tanya's not quite right."

"Tanya Mayhall is not quite right to *babysit*?" Rachel had walked up and heard him. Her skepticism mirrored Honey's. "She's perfect."

Again Cole shrugged, helpless and irritated. "Support me on this. Please." After a glance between them, they nodded.

Cole retrieved Tanya's teacup and brought it to the kitchen. Honey took it from him. The second her fingers touched his, he stepped away. She did the same thing. He wasn't a skittish kind of man. She wasn't a jumpy woman.

Whew. This situation was getting on everyone's nerves.

"Who did you book next?" Honey asked.

"Ellen Clarkson."

Rachel nodded along with Honey. "Another good possibility," she said.

Cole sat near the window again, exhausted but with two more interviews still to conduct.

After sitting with her fingers splayed like frog digits until the polish dried, Madeline climbed out of the cave and ran to the window.

In the sunlight, her nails sparkled. He'd be surprised if they were any longer than a quarter of an inch from cuticle to tip.

Her fragility, her utter dependence on him, sent him trembling with insecurity. He glanced at Evan. Cole saw vulnerability there, too. Their losses were huge.

Give him a bunch of bad guys to round up and throw into jail. Give him a fistfight to resolve with his own fists if necessary, or a gun to face down, but not, *not* this.

Madeline held her hands out to Cole. He lifted her onto his lap with the care deserving of a glass ornament and admired the paint job before placing a soft kiss on her forehead and holding her close, his cheek on her tiny head. An aching tenderness swept through him.

When Vy and Chelsea left to head home, Cole hugged them goodbye.

Ellen arrived moments later.

Again, Cole stood through another hug. He loved his townspeople. He loved these women, but their sympathy ripped off countless bandages, tearing open his wounds.

When the time was decent enough, he set her away from him. He asked Honey to sit in on the interview.

Small and elfin, Ellen had a perky way about her that might appeal to the children.

"Hi," she said to the kids inside the cave. "I'm Ellen."

Madeline turned her face into a pillow, refusing to look at the woman, let alone acknowledge her.

Evan drummed his feet. "Hi!"

Cole sat down with Ellen while the children resumed their quiet play in the cave. Too quiet.

Again, as with Tanya, he covered the basics, then moved on to, "How would you fill your time with the children?"

"Play! We'd do lots of fun stuff."

Yes! Fun stuff sounded good.

"Like what?"

"We'd get outside every day, rain or shine. Children shouldn't be indoors. Ever. Unless they're sleeping. They should be involved in physical activity. Tires them out."

"But you'd have quiet time indoors, too, right?"

"Don't see why I should. Raised all of my kids to enjoy the outdoors. You know Karen's being considered for the Olympic ski team? Downhill racing. Richard's studying to be a phys-ed teacher. Football's his specialty. Likes to coach. Thinks all kids need to be physically active. I taught him that."

But Evan loved to read comic books and do puzzles. Madeline liked to play with dolls and jigsaw puzzles with huge cardboard or wooden pieces. Cole knew that much about them.

"But—"

Ellen talked over him. "Kids need to be outdoors, Cole. You have to understand how important that is."

He foresaw arguments. Yes, children needed to be outdoors, especially with summer so close, but even when it rained? He wanted them out swimming and playing at the splash pad the town had set up in the park.

But *all* the time?

He thanked Ellen for coming out and told her he'd be in touch.

"Think of what I said, Cole. Outdoors. Important. Necessary."

She bent to give Madeline a kiss on her cheek, despite her cool reception on her arrival.

Madeline turned her back to Ellen. In other circumstances, the action would have been almost comical.

"I can fix that with plenty of play," Ellen said, ignoring the fact that the child had just lost her parents.

He nodded and closed the door behind her, trudging back upstairs to face Honey and Rachel.

They watched him silently.

He shook his head.

"I agree, Cole," Honey said. "She's not right. Not for Evan and Madeline. Not at this time, at any rate."

Cole exhaled. He hadn't wanted Honey to fight him on this.

He'd been dropped into an alternate-reality version of Goldilocks.

Tanya was too hard. Studies. For a three-and-a-half-year-old. Well, maybe not according to Honey, but in Cole's mind? Yeah. Give the child another year.

Or maybe not. It was only reading. God, he didn't *know*!

But compared to Ellen's stringent approach, maybe Tanya was too soft.

Would Maria Tripoli be just right? He'd know in—he checked his watch—twenty minutes.

Half an hour later, he watched Maria leave and knew she was pretty darn close to what he needed. Not too hard, not too soft. But perfect?

He couldn't decide.

Was there such a thing where Evan and Madeline were concerned?

Madeline had resisted overtures from even affectionate, nonthreatening Maria. If Maria couldn't physically touch her, how could she care for her?

Honey and Rachel watched him.

What could he say?

I can't hire these women because I can't give these children over to anyone but myself?

Unreasonable. He had to work. His deputies could cover for the coming week, no problem, but that was it. He'd taken off suddenly last week, and they'd filled in for him. But now he needed to get back to his job.

In one week, he would need this settled.

Tori peeked her head out of the cave.

"Honey, can we have snacks?"

"*Again?* You want food *again?*"

Madeline looked stricken by her tone, but Tori giggled, seeing right through Honey's phony indignation. "We're hungry already, Honey."

"Okay. Let's see what else Vy brought for us."

"Can we have crackers and jam, Honey?"

"What makes you think I have all of that, missy?"

"You always haves them for me."

Honey burst out laughing, her smile a slash of rich sunshine on a cloudy day. God, she brightened his spirits.

Cole basked in her reflected glow, trying to convince himself yet again that it was enough just to be near her. That he didn't need more. That her good cheer was worth taking a risk when his past shouted, *Don't do it, fool! You know better.*

He'd arrived in town fourteen years ago with a few bucks in his pocket and not much else. Honey had been a budding teenager, fourteen at a guess, and far too young for him to even notice.

He'd come from a bad and aching place. He'd put it all behind himself and had flourished here in Rodeo, working in law enforcement.

Four years later, when she'd been old enough for him not only to notice but to fall for hard, Cole found he couldn't utter a full sentence that made a damned bit of sense when Honey was around.

She tied his brain and his tongue into knots.

Honey brought out all of his old insecurities.

By then, there'd also been Daniel in her life, and Cole had lost all hope.

Seven years ago, Daniel had died. Not well or easily. Cole had witnessed it and, at Daniel's request, had lied to Honey about aspects of it. Cole could never forget his role in that cover-up.

Honey had been inconsolable for a long time.

Six years ago, she'd lost her mother. He'd had no soothing words or caring hugs. He'd overcome a lot of the damage his parents had done to him, but not when it came to Honey.

Even an expression of condolence had been more than he could make.

The only way Cole had found to ease her pain was to help at the bar on the weekends. She and her mother had been a real team. Honey had grown up in this apartment over the bar her mother had named for her, hoping that someday her daughter would take it over. As soon as Honey was old enough, she had started to work there. When her mother died, she had inherited the bar.

Cole had stopped in on the first Friday night after her mother's death, intending to do nothing more than make sure Honey was okay.

At that time, she hadn't been used to running the place without her mother there. When Honey had needed a break, Cole had stepped behind the bar and filled in.

Nothing had been said, by him or by her.

Somehow, he'd just kept going back.

Those Friday and Saturday nights were bittersweet torture, but he wouldn't give them up for anything.

Honey bent over Tori, laughing. "I do always have

crackers for you, don't I?" she said. A curtain of Honey's blond curls covered Tori.

Madeline's tiny fingers inched forward and grabbed it. Automatically, Honey picked her up. Madeline nestled into her arms and into the shield of her hair.

"Everyone to the table," Honey ordered. "No crunchy crackers on my furniture, if you please."

They climbed onto the chairs and settled in to wait.

Honey pulled out a box of saltines, buttered them and spread a little raspberry jam on each.

She put plates of crackers in front of the children.

Tori turned to kneel on the chair, grasping the rungs on the back and threw her arms around Honey. "I love you."

Honey bussed her loudly on her puckered lips. "I love you, too, Tori-ori-ori-o."

Madeline turned around to kneel on her chair and stare at Honey.

About to return to the kitchen, Honey stopped, arrested. She glanced at Cole, unsure what to do. He didn't know, either.

He held his breath.

Sure, Madeline had allowed Honey to hold her, but this went way past that.

Madeline stretched her tiny arms toward Honey and pursed her tiny mouth.

Honey approached cautiously and touched her lips to the rosebud mouth.

When she eased away, she said, "Thank you, Maddy-addy-addy-o."

For a protracted moment, Madeline stared solemnly before scrambling around on her chair and sitting down. She picked up one cracker and took a tiny bite. It crumbled into her lap. Her lower lip wobbled.

Honey said, "No problem. Those crackers do that all the time."

"To me, too, Honey. Remember before?" Tori asked.

Honey brushed off the crumbs and threw them into the garbage. She pushed Madeline closer to the table and drew the plate right under her chin.

"There. Now the crumbs will fall onto the plate."

Evan sat quietly watching it all. Cole crouched beside him and asked, "How're you doing?"

The child mumbled, "Okay," but Cole hadn't missed the longing while he watched Honey's interplay with the girls.

Honey's keen eye caught it all. Cole should have known she would.

When the children finished, Honey brought a damp washcloth over to wipe their hands. She started with Evan and made a fuss over him, so much so his cheeks turned red. Still crouched on his other side, Cole felt the same impulse Madeline had felt when Honey's hair fell forward.

He itched to run his fingers through it. Over the years, he'd wondered if it was as soft as it looked.

Next, Honey finished with Madeline, who let her clean her jam-sticky hands.

Madeline turned over her hands and held them in front of Honey.

"Yes, I noticed your lovely nails. Chelsea did a fabuloso job, didn't she?"

Madeline nodded and Cole sighed.

The child had accepted Honey through and through.

She was letting Honey touch her.

She had let Honey kiss her.

Cole stared, shattered by a realization he should have seen sooner.

Honey would make an excellent caregiver. The children's new nanny had to be Honey.

She might not be right for *him*, but she was perfect for the children.

There wasn't a doubt in his mind that it *had* to be Honey.

Well, yeah, one doubt—a big one—her work. Her bar. But otherwise, she was perfect as a nanny. Surely, they could work it out *somehow*?

"Honey?"

She glanced over her shoulder from the kitchen where she rinsed the washcloth.

"Could I talk to you?" Gesturing with his head toward the hallway, he stepped forward.

With a questioning brow, she preceded him toward the back of the apartment, away from little ears.

"Rachel," Cole murmured, "watch the kids?"

"Of course."

Now to convince Honey, a woman who ran a busy and successful business, that he needed her to take care of his children.

It might look like selfishness on his part, but no. It was all about Evan and Madeline.

Honey stepped into her bedroom and Cole halted at the doorway, not sure he wanted to get close to her here. Even so small an intimacy threatened him, especially now, in this time of vulnerable need.

Whatever he had expected should he ever step into Honey Armstrong's bedroom, it wasn't this.

Charcoal walls closed in the space, making the large room small and cozy. White linen and lace everywhere brightened things. The startling contrast worked.

With Honey's take-charge character, he hadn't expected lace. Sure, she wore a lot of fancy turquoise-and-silver jewelry and leaned toward off-the-shoulder white tops, but making love to her here would be like bedding down in a big bowl of confectioners' sugar.

It would be amazing.

Honey stood beside her bed, and Cole swallowed. It sounded loud in the quiet room.

Because he'd dreamed so many times of making love to

Honey, he stayed where he was in the doorway, far away from all of that feminine lace and fancy wrought iron.

Had the bed been made for her? It was unique enough. Cole could see Honey sketching out what she wanted and having it styled just for her, controlling every minute particle of her life.

Above the bed hung a huge abstract landscape painting in purples, reds and silver. Another contrast. Honey and her passion in oil on canvas.

Had the artist known her?

The name came to him quickly. Local artist Zachary Brandt, whose landscapes hung all over town. None of them was like this one, though. He'd nailed Honey. Metaphorically, at least. Cole hoped they'd never had a relationship, especially not in this very room.

Cole liked the guy. He didn't want to harbor feelings of jealousy.

Honey cocked her head. "You wanted to talk?"

"Yeah, uh…" He didn't have a clue how to broach the subject, so he blurted, "I want you for the children."

"What do you mean?"

"I want *you* to be their nanny."

Chapter Four

"What?" In her shock, Honey's voice came out strident.

She had to have heard Cole wrong. He had *not* just asked her to be his nanny.

Not that there was anything wrong with the job. In other circumstances, it would be perfect for her, particularly because she loved children.

But she also loved her business, the bar she ran so well. What on earth was the man thinking?

"You can't be serious, Cole."

"I am."

He took on that expression of stubborn force she'd seen in the bar when he dealt with drunks. Cole was an easygoing guy until you crossed him. Then he wanted his way.

The guy could be so rigid. It made him a good sheriff. He kept the town in line even as everyone respected him. But now was not the time for obstinacy.

"There was absolutely nothing wrong with Maria Tripoli," she argued.

Cole leaned an arm up high on the doorjamb and cocked a hip. The man sure knew how to look attractive, but his charms didn't work on her when he was suggesting something so outrageous.

"Maria was good," he said, as though making a big concession. "She's a nice lady, but—"

He chewed on his lower lip, his frustration evident along with his exhaustion.

"But?" Honey prompted.

"Madeline won't let her touch her."

Ah. "So I'm deemed adequate because I could get her to let me wipe her hands clean?"

"She lets you hold her."

"True, but that's just because of my hair. You said that reminds her of her mother."

Silent for so long Honey thought he wouldn't answer, Cole finally responded with emotion thickening his voice. "It was the kiss."

"Oh." Honey considered that. "But why is that so important?"

"She let you wipe her hands and hold her, but she asked for the kiss."

"Okay, so?" Honey's frustration edged into her voice.

"So, not one single woman has been able to touch her except you. Not her grandmother or women who were friends with my sister and who Madeline knew well. Since the accident and all during the funeral, she wouldn't let any other women hold her."

Cole held her gaze, as though to get her to agree with him by sheer force of will. "She didn't *let* you kiss her," he repeated. "She *asked* for it."

She pointed toward the floor, indicating the bar downstairs. "What about my business?"

"I don't know, Honey. I guess my concern is the child. It's a huge thing to ask, but it's not for me. Madeline responded to you. It's for the children. Both of them. Evan doesn't show it, but he needs affection, too."

Honey was drawn to little girls, but she had noticed Evan's longing and made a note to give him more attention.

"I don't know what to do with them, Honey."

All his grief, all the weight of his dilemma and burden ravaged his face.

"Were you close to your sister?"

"She was my salvation."

Salvation. Strong word. "What do you mean?"

His gaze slid away from her to the fist he pounded gently against the doorjamb. "I don't want to talk about it."

She'd never heard a whisper about his past. Cole had a right to his privacy. She wouldn't push it, but *salvation* signified huge feelings.

She could feel his pain, but she couldn't see how she could take care of the children and still run the bar.

"Okay, listen, this is what we'll do. Tomorrow you'll have to interview more nannies until you find one. I can't be it, Cole."

In his expression disappointment transmuted into acceptance. He exhaled roughly. "Will you take care of them while I talk to more people?"

"I can't. We have Rib Fest in front of the bar through lunch."

Cole groaned. "I forgot about that. Do you have to do it?"

"It's a fund-raiser for the revival of the fair and rodeo. I have a ton of ribs marinating downstairs. Chet's coming in this evening to boil them."

He knocked his fist against the doorjamb again. She could see his mind working.

"No." She preempted him. "I will not leave Chet to take care of it alone. He'll be cooking all morning and serving for two hours over lunch. We presold hundreds of tickets. It's our biggest fund-raiser yet."

He opened his mouth, closed it.

"You're being unreasonable in your need and shock, Cole. Don't ask me to cancel or abandon Chet."

He hung his head. "You're right, of course."

"I can enlist my friends to help with them. While that's happening, you interview more women to find someone who's just right."

"What if no one else can get through to Madeline? So far, it's only you, Honey."

"Don't use guilt on me, Cole. I don't appreciate it. I'll spend as much spare time as I can with Madeline, but you have to find someone who can care for the children full-time. Okay?"

Cole nodded, but she wasn't at all certain she'd gotten through to him.

"I mean it, Cole. I expect you to put in your best effort to find someone else."

"I will," he promised, and she believed him.

A tiny head peered around Cole's legs—Madeline, her blue eyes a miniature version of her uncle's, but large in her tiny face. Every bit as haunted as his, they softened Honey's defenses, and that would not do.

She couldn't offer everything Cole needed, but she would give as much as she could.

Madeline stared at the bed, took one step forward, changed her mind and retreated to hide against Cole's leg.

"You want to get up on it?" Cole asked.

The tiny head, face pressed against Cole's knee, nodded.

The girl approached and touched the lace on Honey's pillowcase.

COLE STEPPED FORWARD and lifted Madeline up onto all of Honey's lace. A photo on the bedside table caught his eye.

Daniel, with the devil in his bright eyes and a cheeky grin. Still in her bedroom. Still in her heart?

Cole had lied to Honey about Daniel.

He frowned and tried to shake off the old guilt, but couldn't.

Maddy snuggled into the middle of Honey's five lace-covered pillows, stuck her thumb into her mouth and closed her eyes.

"Oh!" Honey exclaimed. "We need to get her settled into wherever she'll be sleeping tonight."

Cole realized the same thing. He picked up Madeline, whose eyes shot open. She stared wide-eyed at him and back at the bed, chin wobbling.

"Let's go home," he said then grimaced when Madeline looked hopeful.

"To your new home," he qualified.

Expression settling into resignation, she rubbed her head against Cole's shoulder.

Darling, you're breaking my heart.

Honey swore under her breath. Cole felt the same way. No child should have to face such harsh reality.

Honey led them out of the bedroom and down the hallway to the living room.

"We're going to take the children to Cole's apartment and get them settled in," she told Rachel, who sat on the sofa nursing Beth under a blanket. Evan and Tori played quietly in the cave.

"May I make a suggestion?" Rachel adjusted her daughter beneath the blanket.

"What's that?" Cole asked.

"Why don't you and Honey go over and get everything set up first while I watch the children?"

"Good idea," Cole said, so close behind Honey his breath ruffled her hair. He stepped away to lay Madeline down at the opposite end of the sofa and snagged an afghan to cover her.

"We'll be back soon," he said.

Honey headed downstairs, and Cole followed.

They stepped into sunshine painting Main Street bright and sharp. Families wandered the street toward the park at the far end or drove through town at a leisurely Sunday pace as though this were a normal day, as though Cole hadn't brought home two children today.

Across the road and down a few stores, Cole unlocked the door to his apartment above the cop shop. They climbed a narrow staircase that opened into a living room.

Cole wandered the room turning on lamps, because, despite the sunny day, not a lot of sunshine leaked in through the small window.

He studied his place as though through Honey's eyes.

She wasn't judgmental, but would she note that he hadn't done much to make it a home despite having been here for years?

Serviceable furniture lined the walls. One big slab of a coffee table dominated the center of the narrow room as a catchall for remote controls and magazines. The latest Jack Reacher novel lay open facedown. He'd started it a month ago.

A television mounted on the wall had a layer of dust on its surface.

No wonder he spent his weekends at Honey's Place, where there was plenty of laughter and warmth, to get away from this nothingness that he couldn't call home.

"Come here," he said.

Bypassing his small, clean kitchen, Honey trailed him down a cramped hallway past a suitcase he'd dropped before bringing the children and their backpacks to the bar.

They passed his miniscule bathroom to arrive at his bedroom at the end of the hallway.

Apart from a king-size bed and a dresser, there wasn't much space left for anything else.

The bed, unmade and littered with clothing, told the story of that awful phone call and his mad dash to Oregon for the funeral.

Hands on hips, Honey said, "This apartment is tiny. Where are you going to put the children?"

"In here. I'll put on fresh sheets."

"Where will you sleep?"

"On the sofa."

Honey marched back to the living room and stared at the leather sofa, big and puffy and at least a dozen years out of date. He might not be able to stretch out full-length, but it would do until he could figure a better housing solution.

"You're going to be uncomfortable," Honey said.

"Yeah."

"You know this isn't the best spot for them."

"I know. I'll have to, I don't know, buy a house, I guess."

"But in the meantime…" Honey glanced around. "It's so dim in here. Is it always like this?"

"Uh-huh. It's not the greatest place, but the price is right as long as I'm sheriff."

"I can't believe you've stayed here all these years."

"The town likes to have me close to the office."

"I understand, but they should have done more to make it better. A larger window would have been a good idea."

"I guess. I don't spend a lot of time here, Honey. I'm in the bar or at the diner, or I visit friends. The rest of the time I'm at work or the gym."

"I understand, Cole, but have you given a thought to how unsuitable this place is? It's dark and depressing."

Cole followed the arc of her outstretched arm. "I'll buy a house. I'll check out what's available with the real estate office. In the meantime, they have to stay with me."

"Now that we're away from the children," she said, "tell me the full story."

He ground his teeth. He didn't want to go through it all again.

"What happened to your sister and her husband?" He knew Honey wouldn't let it go until he'd told. She should know it all anyway, so she would understand the children's behavior.

"Car accident," he said, folding his lips in tight. *Don't break down.*

Honey said, "Thank God the children weren't involved."

Here came the worst part. *Breathe.* "They were there."

Honey stilled. "What do you mean?"

"They were in the car. In the backseat."

Her hand went to her throat. "Were either of them injured?"

"Not physically, but…" Cole shoved his hands into his pockets and hunched his shoulders against the pain of the telling. "It was on a back road near where they lived. At night. Not a lot of traffic. It took a while for someone to come upon them and to call emergency services. When they arrived, it was already too late."

In his mind's eye, Cole saw it all—the children unable to rouse their parents, the silence, the darkness, the fear.

He would do anything to make up for the loss Evan and Madeline had suffered. He would do his best, but he worried.

He stared at Honey. Of course, his request that she be their nanny had been unreasonable, but he swore he'd use every persuasion in his arsenal for the children if he thought he could get away with it.

He huffed out a breath. "I need to bring those children here and get them settled in for bedtime."

"It's been a hellish week for you." Honey rested her hand on Cole's shoulder, startling him.

"Yeah." Cole edged away to stare out the window. Honey's touch did magical, forbidden things to him.

"They could stay with me for tonight. Would you object? I have a spare room. They can share a bed."

Cole's feelings shuttered faster than a home in tornado alley ahead of an oncoming twister. He'd like nothing better—not for the children, but for himself. *He* wanted to stay in that warm apartment suffused with Honey's personality. He could let the children stay there, but he couldn't bring himself to be away from them.

"Only for tonight and maybe tomorrow night, too," she said. "Just until you find a better solution."

"No."

"Why not?" she asked.

"Don't ask me to be that far away from them. I don't want that. I don't think they would want it, either."

"You can sleep on my sofa. It has to be more comfortable than this." She pointed to his leather behemoth. "At least you can stretch out on mine."

"They're my responsibility now." Cole turned to the window to tamp down the temptation running rampant through his veins. "When I got to town today, I walked in here with them and panicked. I didn't want to be alone with them when I don't have a clue what to do with them. That's why I showed up at your place. You're fun. Lighthearted. I thought they would get along with you and like you. They do."

He hardened himself against his own desire to give in to weakness. "I'm their new guardian. This is their new life. I need to take care of them."

"Okay."

He didn't move, but his gaze shifted around the apartment, to the hollowness of the place. To the lack of character and warmth.

Honey didn't speak. She wasn't here to make his decisions for him. That was his job.

"You know," he said, chest hollow, "I really don't want to stay here. I've stood on my own two feet since leaving home years ago, but tonight—"

Pain filled, anger rising, he picked up a book from a table and threw it across the room.

His rough impulse startled Honey.

"Sorry." A heavy breath whooshed out of him. "Sorry. I'm angry. Those kids… They deserve better than this. Than me."

"Better than you? What on earth do you mean?"

"They need someone who knows how to be a father."

"Cole, you're about as dependable as anyone I've ever met. You need time to adjust to this huge change in your life and to learn how to be a parent. Don't expect perfection from yourself right out of the gate."

"They deserve better than this dark old place." He tried not to hyperventilate. He should take what she offered, just to make his job easier for this one lousy night before more reality than he could handle came crashing down on him.

"Just for tonight," he said. "We'll stay for one night, okay?"

"Of course," she said. "I want to help, Cole. You know that."

He placed his hand on her arm with a tenderness in the touch his discipline seldom allowed him to feel.

He rarely touched her and yet, he sat in Honey's Place every Friday and Saturday night, on the stool at the bar that the other patrons left empty and waiting for him no matter how crowded the place became.

Everyone knew that Cole would show up as soon as he'd finished work for the day.

He would sit on that stool and nurse two beers before ordering a bacon double cheeseburger with fries for dinner. When the beers were gone, he would switch to root beer for the rest of the night.

At the moment, his hand still rested on her arm.

It was only relief and gratitude, but his fingers tingled where he touched the skin of her arm.

A highway of nerve endings, of pure sensation, shot from her to him.

He dropped his hand and sat on the sofa, where he leaned his elbows on his knees and cradled his head.

"What a mess." He laughed bitterly. "I never expected this in my life. I love those children, but I can't believe they're mine now."

He swiped his hand across his mouth, where despair backed up in his throat. How the *hell* was he supposed to raise those two little beings? "I know how to track down criminals. I know how to keep the townspeople safe. I know how to testify in court to the best of my abilities, but how am I supposed to do *this*?"

"Buck up, Cole." Honey's stern voice stiffened his spine. "We'll figure this out."

He liked the sound of that *we*.

From this moment, he would be responsible for Evan and Madeline. He would be the one teaching them. He would be their sole source and provider of every single little thing, both physical and emotional.

Lord, he'd have to teach them table manners, how to eat properly, how to speak well, how to dress, how to…

Enough. He was getting ahead of himself. First he had to get through today.

When he stood, Honey did the oddest thing. She unbuttoned his shirt and re-buttoned it, the action intimate and wifely. He stifled a gasp because the woman was offering temptation on a platter. He should move away. He couldn't.

She didn't touch his skin, but when she finished and patted his shirt as though he were a child, there was *nothing* childish about his response.

Like wrestling a steer, he wrangled his unruly desires under control, just barely, mindful of how much he had to keep his distance from Honey, and yet…he needed her for the children.

"That's been bothering me since you walked into the

bar. Now it's buttoned properly," she murmured, seemingly unaware of her effect on him. "When did you last sleep?"

He released the breath he'd been holding. "Don't remember."

"You need as much taking care of as the children."

He hadn't wanted to admit it to himself, but yeah, he did. He'd been independent, on his own, since he'd turned twenty-one.

He was a strong man. Most people who knew him would say he had backbone and solid ethics, but taking on responsibility for two tiny humans scared the shit out of him.

His turmoil must have shown. Honey ordered, "Calm down."

How? With Sandy gone, his family was gone. The only family that mattered, that is. He didn't count the woman who'd given birth to the two of them and the man who'd fathered them, both of whom had shown up at the funeral and been angry when the will had been read and they'd been denied the right to take the children home with them.

As if reading his thoughts, Honey asked, "Are there no other relatives who can help to raise them?"

"Dennis grew up in foster care and had no family left that he knew of. Mine—Sandy's—well… Sandy and Dennis willed the children's care to me." And that was the end of that.

Maybe trying to lighten the heavy atmosphere, Honey said, "At least we don't have to worry about diapers."

Cole hadn't thought of that. He shuddered. Thank God, they weren't babies.

But he'd heard that *we* again. He tried to smile back. "There is that in our favor."

He opened the suitcase he'd brought from Sandy's home, but there was nothing in it he would need overnight. The children had their pajamas and toothbrushes in their backpacks, so they were ready to sleep anywhere. They didn't seem to want to part with them.

Maybe the bags offered security or something. Along with the normal everyday items, they also held some of their favorite small toys.

From the bedroom, he got himself a pair of sweatpants and a T-shirt to sleep in. He snagged his toiletries bag.

Ready to head back to her place, he found Honey in the living room staring outside. He might not want to let himself get close to her, but she was a good person, doing so much for them.

He said, "You're kindhearted, Honey."

She turned around and blinked. He understood why. He never said nice things to her. He didn't speak to her much. He couldn't, not when his default action before today had been to become tongue-tied the second she was in his vicinity.

He was a smart guy, but he became a fool where Honey Armstrong was concerned.

Not at the moment, though. Not completely. Not when he needed her help so badly.

"Should I bring my sleeping bag?"

"No. I have plenty of blankets."

They trudged down the stairs, back across the street and upstairs to Honey's apartment.

Rachel waited for them. "We have to leave now to be home in time for dinner with Travis."

Rachel and Honey hugged. Honey held Beth while Rachel put on a sweater and wrapped her arms around Cole. "Take care of yourself, okay?"

Cole nodded against the top of her head.

He'd never known such good people, had such great friends, before coming to Rodeo, Montana.

"'Bye, Sheriff Cole," Tori piped up. He patted her head.

"Goodbye, Evan and Madeline," Rachel said. "When

you get more settled in, come to our house for a visit, okay?"

Evan nodded hard. "Yeah!"

Madeline stared.

They left with Honey following to lock the front door, taking every semblance of normality with them.

Cole stared at his two young charges. Terror opened huge cracks in his normally rock-solid self-confidence as he stood alone with them in this room.

He was lost.

Chapter Five

Honey returned upstairs to find Cole still hovering just inside the door.

Honey's apartment was spacious. Cole made it feel small.

The thought of him sleeping in her apartment made her nerves skitter. Weird. She believed without a doubt that Cole would never in a kajillion years make an advance.

So why are you nervous, Honey?

Because all of these years while Honey had been thinking of him as just the town sheriff, she'd ignored how truly beautiful the man was. She'd *made* herself ignore it, because she didn't want to find him attractive.

He worked in one of the most dangerous careers on the planet—law enforcement.

Daniel's death as a young deputy killed on the job had taught her that powerful lesson. Never again would she be involved with a lawman. There was too much pain at the end of that road.

Don't think about it, Honey. Move on.

Here in her apartment, Cole was too big and too male—and made her edgy just standing in her space.

She went to the kitchen to prepare dinner, to do anything to stay away from Cole.

She'd made that mistake of re-buttoning his shirt, of standing too close to his heat, and it had felt wonderful.

So, the solution was to keep her distance and be as normal as possible.

She put together their dinner—leftover roast beef and scalloped potatoes.

"Seems all we've been doing is eating since we got here," Cole said.

"The roast is incredibly tender." Honey cut Madeline's into tiny bites.

"Yeah." Cole moved the food around on his plate.

"Thank goodness for Vy and her diner food," Honey said, trying to lighten the heaviness in the room, to keep the silence that threatened to overwhelm them all at bay.

"Uh-huh." Cole seemed to have settled into monosyllables again.

After dinner, Honey made up her long, comfy L-shaped sofa with a pillow and a couple of quilts for Cole.

Honey was all about hominess and comfort. When she wasn't dealing with the busyness of owning a business and corralling rowdy cowboys ready to have fun on the weekend, she liked to nest.

She started to pull apart the child cave to straighten up for the night, but Evan protested.

"I like it," he said. More importantly, he added, "Madeline likes it, too." In other words, big brother was taking care of his little sister.

Honey left it intact.

Together, but also apart, Honey and Cole got the children ready for bed.

Honey bathed Madeline and dressed her in a small flannel nightshirt.

Cole gave Evan a bath. The child emerged with damp hair, wearing a pair of Star Wars pajamas.

Both subdued children brushed their teeth.

There was no hint there would be fireworks until they tried to put Evan into bed in the spare room.

"I want to sleep with Cole." With a mulish jut of his sharp little jaw, he crossed his arms and refused to stay on the bed.

"There's a perfectly good bed right here for you and your sister," Cole said.

"No!"

Evan unleashed a torrent of noes and twists and turns to evade Cole's efforts to keep him in the bed.

Cole sighed. "Evan, there's no need for you to sleep on the sofa."

"Would it be so bad, Cole?" Honey asked. "Just for tonight?"

"It's not just tonight. It's been every night."

Honey understood immediately. He was exhausted. He needed a good night's sleep on his own.

"Get in the bed," Cole said, not unkindly.

Evan backed himself into the corner of the room. "No, no, no!" he shouted. He sat down and kicked his feet on the floor in a full-blown tantrum.

Honey stared at Cole. "Has he been like this since the funeral?"

"No. He's been quiet. We were still in his parents' house."

"When did you leave there?"

"This morning."

"So tonight he's in a strange apartment in a different town, even a different state, and being asked to sleep in a bed that's not his. And all he wants is his parents, no doubt."

Cole picked up Evan and put him on the bed, but he'd wrapped his arms around Cole and wouldn't let go.

He cried and screamed, even though Cole lay down beside him, setting off Madeline.

Honey picked her up and carried her into her own bedroom, closing the door to block out Evan's screams as much as she could.

It wasn't her business to tell Cole how to parent these children. Evan needed to be with Cole. Cole needed sleep.

The man was stuck between a rock and a hard place.

Honey figured her role right now was to take care of Madeline for a few minutes, to give Cole room to work things out with Evan.

She stepped out of her slippers and climbed into bed, awkwardly, because Madeline wouldn't ease her grip.

Oh, these vulnerable, hurting children. So much pain.

Honey arranged the pillows across the headboard and sat up against them with Madeline in her arms across her lap. She snugged the white eyelet lace comforter up around the child and started to hum to try to drown out Evan.

Madeline cried.

Honey poured all of her soothing grace and care into her hold on the child, pressing her close.

She hummed and hummed.

Madeline's sobs quieted in time and became hiccups. Gradually, she fell asleep.

Honey held her tightly, afraid that she would wake again. Madeline needed sleep.

In time, the noise from the other room stopped.

A short while later, her door opened quietly on its well-oiled hinges. Cole peeked in.

"Is he asleep?" Honey whispered.

"Yeah. Finally. Madeline?"

She nodded.

He stepped into the room. "I'll take her to her bed."

Gingerly, he took Madeline from Honey without waking her.

She said quietly, "I left you a bath towel and a washcloth in the bathroom. Why don't you get washed up after you put Madeline to bed?"

He nodded and left. Honey heard him enter the spare bedroom, and then a minute later, the faucet turned on in the bathroom. Madeline must have stayed asleep when he put her in the spare bed with Evan.

Ten minutes later, Honey cleaned up for the night. The living room was dark, as was the spare bedroom.

She went to her room and left her door ajar. She needed to hear the children when they awoke in the morning so she could make breakfast.

Cole must have been exhausted. Even from here, Honey could hear the faint rumbles of his snores.

She said goodnight to Daniel's photograph, as she did every night, patted it and pulled up her covers.

Lying in bed, staring through the crack in the curtains to the ambient light of the town reflecting from the sky, she tried to remember the last time she'd had a man sleeping in her apartment.

She fell asleep still trying to remember.

Honey awoke in the middle of the night to silence.

She checked the time. Two a.m.

So why had she awakened?

A small sound drifted down the hallway—a child sobbing, followed by a deep voice consoling.

Honey threw off her covers and tiptoed to the living room.

Rumpled, Cole sat with Madeline curled against his chest crying, the floor lamp beside him casting yellow light over them. Evan snuggled under one of his arms, hiccuping.

Cole looked tired still. Four hours wasn't enough to overcome his past week.

Honey approached. "What can I do?"

After a quick glance at her bare legs—nuts, she'd forgotten to put on a robe to cover her oversize T-shirt—he said, "I don't know. They don't like to be alone in the dark."

While Cole might ooze masculine vitality in his everyday life, at this moment darkness banded his eyes and shadowed their depths.

"Too quiet." Evan hiccuped some more.

Honey's stereo system sat in the far corner. She turned it on and found an easy listening station, adjusting the volume down to barely audible, nothing more than white noise in the background.

From the guest room she retrieved their pillows. Cole needed sleep in whatever way possible.

Stopping in the kitchen, she turned on the light over the stove.

Back in the living room, she said, "Evan, come to this end of the sofa. You can sleep here. Okay?"

Evan nodded, and Honey set up a cozy nest of a pillow and a couple of afghans on the short end of the L. He crawled over, and she tucked him in.

"Here," she said, handing Cole a pillow. "Lie down with her on your chest. When she falls asleep, you can move her over beside you with her own pillow."

"Good thinking." Cole untangled the blankets that were half underneath them.

When he settled onto his back, Madeline curled on top of his warm, T-shirt-covered chest, closed her eyes and put her thumb into her mouth.

Honey tucked the blankets around both of them.

Before she could leave, Cole grasped her arm, his long fingers wrapping around her wrist.

The warmth of it shot through her.

"Thanks," he said. That was all.

So like Cole to be brief. His eyes said far more. Honey just didn't know how to interpret the message there.

Unsettled by his intensity, she nodded, turned off the

floor lamp to leave only the muted light from the kitchen, and returned to her bedroom. Curled in her own bed, she touched her wrist where she could swear she still felt Cole's heat on her skin.

HONEY AWOKE AT seven the following morning. She walked down the hallway toward the bathroom, yawning widely and wondering whether Cole had gotten much sleep last night.

The closed bathroom door opened just as she got there, revealing Cole stepping out and hauling his T-shirt over his head.

But first—oh, first—she got an eyeful of gorgeous male flesh, an entire broad chest of it. The shoulders and biceps that looked so big in clothing looked even bigger, and better, naked.

His jeans hung low on his hips. There was not one ounce of flab on the man.

The scent of shampoo and soap drifted on a wave of humidity from the small room. He'd already showered. She hadn't heard a thing.

Damp hair stuck to his scalp.

In a perfect world, she would curl against him as she wanted to and wrap her arms around his warm tempting body.

Mentally, she took a sharp step away from those sultry images. She couldn't think about Cole that way.

Mouth dry, she said, "You should have slept in."

"Couldn't."

Her brows rose. "Too bad."

He finished pulling his shirt to his waist, hiding the tempting breadth of him. Honey hoped he hadn't noticed her interest. There was nowhere for it to go.

It had been a long time since she'd had sex. Honey liked men. She liked their bodies.

Nothing would happen with Cole, though, because she refused to let anything come of her attraction to a man in law enforcement.

But that chest. That wonderful, manly perfection.

Why couldn't they have found a way for him to sleep at his own place so she wouldn't wander down her hallway this morning to the shock of Cole Payette's beauty?

Virile—it seemed like an old-fashioned word these days, but it fit Cole. He was pure temptation.

Put on your crisp sheriff's uniform. Become the controlled officer. Remind me why you are off-limits.

Don't be a man who tempts me in my own apartment.

Funny that she'd never noticed before how narrow the hallway was, or how little air made its way down here.

Cole's sharp blue gaze watched her, but he said not a word. Typical Cole, Honey thought, but without heat. As much as his silences sometimes bothered her, there was something nice about standing here with him in early morning quiet, as though the rest of the world didn't exist.

He reached up to switch off the bathroom light and dimness enveloped them, making the world even smaller.

Cole turned to head down the hallway back to the quiet living room.

Shaken by her newly awakened and unwelcome awareness of Cole, Honey entered the washroom and closed the door.

She leaned against it and breathed heavily.

Sure, she'd always been aware of how attractive Cole was. How could she not? She had a pair of perfectly good eyes.

But his current proximity rattled her.

Oh, for God's sake, Honey. He's only been in your apartment one night. Pull yourself together.

After that impatient pep talk, she showered and got

herself ready for the day. Before leaving her bedroom, she glanced at Daniel's photograph.

Remember Daniel, Honey. Remember the pain of losing him and resist the handsome sheriff.

By the time she entered the living room, she had her unruly libido under control. Both children were awake and sitting up on the sofa.

Cole stood in her kitchen, the same room that had always felt perfectly spacious to Honey, and consumed all the air.

"I took the liberty of making coffee. Hope you don't mind."

His morning-gruff voice sent shivers along her skin. Pretty sure she had goose bumps, she managed only a nod.

"That's good." She could use a gallon of it.

Evan and Madeline ate cereal inside the afghan-covered armchair fort.

Isolated in their cocoon, they left Honey to share coffee at the breakfast table with Cole while bacon fried on the stove.

A wail erupted from the cocoon, and Cole shot over.

"What's wrong?" He crouched beside the chairs.

"Spilled," a tiny female voice cried.

Honey wasn't worried. Her apartment was made to be used and any problem could be cleaned up or fixed. The damage wouldn't be significant.

"Lady get mad," Madeline wailed.

"No, she won't," Cole said.

"How do you know?" Honey asked. How was he so sure of her?

Honey couldn't interpret the glint in Cole's eye. "I've sat across a bar from you every weekend for six years."

"Yeah. So?"

"I know you." So much certainty in his tone.

Cole removed the afghans and handed Madeline's cereal

bowl to Honey. She took it to the sink, where she dumped it out. The child could have a fresh bowl.

Cole carried Madeline to the spare bedroom.

Honey sponged the milk from the armchair so it wouldn't turn sour. She rinsed her sponge and repeated until it was clean.

Evan sat quietly and watched.

"Are you okay?" Honey asked.

His wary nod didn't reassure her. How unsettled his life must feel right now.

"It's all fine, Evan. Tori once spilled juice on the sofa. It happens."

She kissed his forehead and hugged him. Evan smiled.

Cole came out of the bedroom with Madeline in a fresh top, with the milky one crumpled in his hand.

Honey put it in the sink to soak with a little detergent.

"Better sit at the table this time," Cole said when he'd settled Madeline at the table with fresh cereal and milk.

Evan ran over and joined her. Cole retrieved his cereal bowl from the cave.

He cast Honey a lost look. "I don't know what to do today."

"With the children?" Honey glanced at sunlight streaming through the large front window. "Today is Rib Fest, remember? They'll be busy eating and playing with other children, I'm sure. We have a great day for it."

Cole shook his head. "Sorry. Forgot." She could see that his fuzziness bothered him.

He poured more coffee for both himself and Honey while she fried eggs.

When she'd finished, he took two slices of bacon and put them back into the pan until they were well-done. "They don't like it fatty."

He handed one to Evan and crumbled the other into

small bites on a paper towel, which he set on the table beside Madeline.

After breakfast, Honey washed and dressed the children while Cole cleaned their dishes and pans.

They took the interior back stairs down to the bar, where they found Chet already in the kitchen.

"Hey." He stepped out of the industrial refrigerator. "Who are the kids?"

Cole introduced them and added, "They'll be living with me."

Chet didn't bat an eye. He might be a tall, scary-looking guy with his big belly and tattoo sleeves, but he had a real fondness for children. Plus, he was perceptive enough to realize they all had work to do before the crowds arrived for lunch. He squatted in front of Madeline and Evan. "I got a bunch of brownies that need to be taste tested. Good thing you're here. It can only be done by kids."

God bless Chet, Honey thought, for making the children comfortable.

"You two want to be my official taste testers?" he asked.

Evan nodded so hard a lock of hair fell onto his forehead. Madeline put a thumb into her mouth and nodded, too.

Chet led them to the bar proper and set them up in a booth with cloth bar towels wrapped around their necks like bandannas.

He retrieved two small glasses of milk and two plates. He put a brownie on each one and carried it to the children.

Once he had them all set up, he returned to the kitchen.

"That'll keep 'em for a few minutes," he said. "I'm puttin' you both to work."

Cole hauled folding tables from the big storage shed out behind the parking lot at the back of the building to the curb in front of Honey's Place. His deputies had already cordoned off a section of Main Street for the next few hours.

Chet and Cole rolled out industrial barbecues Honey stored in the same shed. They checked to make sure hoses were clear of spiders and hooked up large propane tanks.

Honey washed the tables and clipped on red-and-white-checked plastic tablecloths.

"It's gonna get hot later," Chet said. "We're in the shade now, but everything will be sunny at high noon."

"You're right," Honey said, "I should have ordered tents."

Cole whipped out his phone and called a friend in the rental business at the other end of the county.

When he finished his conversation, he announced, "We'll have open-sided tents here within the hour."

"I'm impressed." Chet nodded.

Sheriff Payette's normal, capable self had just put in an appearance.

Back in the kitchen, Honey mixed a huge batch of potato salad with the potatoes she'd boiled yesterday morning.

She heard a noise behind her. The children stood with empty plates in their hands.

"We couldn't carry it all," Evan said.

"That's okay. I can get your milk glasses."

"So? What's the verdict?" Chet's big voice boomed from the doorway. "Can I serve those brownies today?"

"Yeah!" Evan jumped from foot to foot. "They were good!"

"Good," Madeline murmured.

So sweet to hear her speak, even if only one word at a time.

Within the hour, volunteers poured in, including the five other members of the Fair and Rodeo Revival Committee, all women.

Vy showed up first with Will, to help with food. They

basted innumerable racks of ribs on the barbecues with Chet's special barbecue sauce, and Vy set up a table with scoured cutting boards where the ribs could be carved when done.

Rachel showed up next with Tori and Beth, to help out with the children. They all gathered indoors until the activities started.

Nadine, a journalist for the local newspaper, the *Rodeo Wrangler*, showed up wearing full makeup, a dress and strappy little sandals. For Rib Fest. So Nadine. So Miss Perfection. She hung Rib Fest banners at the ends of the blockaded portion of the street. At a small table, she collected tickets and sold more if needed.

Samantha Read, Rachel's sister-in-law, arrived with her new husband, Michael, and their four children, two hers and two his. Michael, strong from years of working on his ranch, helped set up the tents.

Last, Max arrived. What could Honey say about Maxine? Max confounded, defied, angered and delighted. A bundle of contradictions, Max was Honey's most confusing friend, but she loved the daylights out of her.

"Give me something to do, Honey," Max ordered in her husky voice.

Honey responded and doled out all kinds of jobs to her army of volunteers, including putting Rachel and Tori in charge of watching Evan and Maddy while Honey and Chet got work done.

Once the crowds arrived at noon, Honey and Chet dispensed drinks and ribs for two solid hours, nonstop.

They'd moved speakers outside, and music blared down Main Street. It was a fund-raiser but also a big, happy party for the whole town.

When Honey had to go inside for more potato salad,

wordlessly and naturally Cole jumped in to sell drinks, as he did in her bar on weekend evenings.

It felt natural and right to do this for Honey.

Chapter Six

Cole settled into a more familiar role with Honey—for a few hours, at least—before the reality of his becoming a guardian kicked in again.

Later, after the ribs were all gone, volunteers helped to dismantle everything and Chet put the barbecues out back to cool down before storing them. Cole moved to carry the speakers inside, but Honey stopped him.

"Look how many kids are here. I want to play with them!"

She put on a CD of children's songs she kept for Tori.

Running into the middle of the street, she yelled, "C'mon, kids, let's dance!"

Cole watched Honey change from business owner to child, the part of her character that disconcerted him.

Honey led about twenty children in a rousing rendition of ring-around-the-rosy with Maddy between her and Tori.

Amazing that she'd persuaded the child to participate.

Honey's white blouse fell off both shoulders. Only then did Cole realize she must be braless. The big white ruffle around the top had hidden any hint of that.

The thought brought desire raging through him. He couldn't remember a time once she'd turned eighteen when he had *not* been aware of Honey's body, of her attractiveness, but being the master of control, he had held it in check.

Sometimes, at moments like this when the sun shone on her waist-length curly blond hair and her smile lit up like a million bucks and her shoulders tempted him to touch, touch, touch and never stop, control was nearly impossible. Yet again, he was forced to admit how much he wanted Honey.

Today she'd dressed in her signature style again.

Her filmy blue skirt floated out around her, flashing glimpses of tanned knees and firm calves. Sunlight glinted from the half dozen thin silver bracelets on each arm.

Earth mother.

Moon goddess.

An overgrown child playing children's games in the middle of Main Street.

The flash of her eyes and her laughter—God, that infectious laughter—nearly undid him. Nearly made him abandon all of his reasons for resisting the woman.

To bring himself back to sanity, back to reason, he pulled forth every rotten memory he had of Shiloh, a trick he'd used through the years to keep his distance from Honey.

Sure, he should have gotten over Shiloh's betrayal years ago, and he would have if he'd been attracted to anyone other than Honey, but the lessons he'd learned from Shiloh served him well at moments like this.

Twenty-one and itching to break free of his parents' stifling dominance, Cole had met Shiloh in a bar near the college he'd attended. She'd bowled him over with her carefree spirit, the antithesis of the iron-solid walls of discipline and control his mother had erected in every area of his life. And in Sandy's, too.

A shining beacon in his otherwise ordered, boring, narrow life, Shiloh had seen easy pickings in Cole.

He'd never known affection and passion and carefree laughter. Shiloh had all of those in spades. He'd never met anyone as free and uninhibited as she.

She'd played him like the innocent, untried fiddle he'd been. Lord, had she played him.

He'd cleaned out his bank accounts and his trust fund in his West Virginia hometown, had left school and hit the road with Shiloh in a beat-up, smoke-belching old Valiant.

When he'd asked where they were headed, her reply had been typical Shiloh—"Sugar, wherever we want."

The thought, the sheer unadulterated nerve of just taking off, had stirred his blood like never before.

He'd thrown back his head and laughed, free at last.

Cole had believed in Shiloh with every cell of his young, naive heart. The wind through the open window of the car had blown her long blond curls all over him. Her filmy dresses had outlined every bone and curve and her unrestrained breasts in the sunlight.

Every moment of every day, he'd ached for the sexual freedom of their nights and often their afternoons, too. Shiloh had been a revelation with her lack of inhibition.

Shiloh had been right about one thing.

It had been past time for him to get out from under his mother's thumb. Until he'd left for college, she had controlled every single aspect of his life, even the courses he'd taken at school and the choice of career, all while his weak-willed father gave in to her every command. Cole no longer wanted his mom's control and he would no longer be his dad.

On a cross-country summer journey of liberty and free love, besotted, Cole had visited music festivals with her, had walked barefoot through farmers' fields, had stolen apples from orchards and had driven in any and all directions.

In motel after motel, during nights of unbridled, carnal passion, he'd professed his love for her.

She'd said the same to him, right up until the morning when he'd awakened to find her gone with the car and every scrap of cash he'd owned. Every cent. Every credit card.

He'd worked off their debt to the motel and had hitched his way across the country. He would never in a million years go back to his parents with his tail between his legs.

Along the way, he'd picked up jobs, had worked hard on farms and ranches until he'd landed in Rodeo, Montana, and had thought, *Here. This is perfect. I'll settle here.*

Once he'd made that decision, he'd continued to work hard on local ranches while he put himself through night school in law enforcement.

After graduation and when he'd become a deputy, his life had calmed down.

He truly had come home.

No way would he allow a free spirit to distract him from the straight and true arrow of his life. No way could he risk having his love betrayed again.

Honey would never steal from him, but she could trample his heart to smithereens. Considering the depth of his love, it wouldn't take much to destroy him.

Honey's laughter lit up Main Street, pulling Cole back to the present and his resolve to withstand his feelings for her.

A couple of years ago, giving in to curiosity, he'd looked up Shiloh in the many databases to which he had access.

She was dead, the victim of a stabbing in a motel room, maybe by someone who hadn't liked being robbed.

She'd never made it to her thirtieth birthday.

He felt sorry that she'd died so young, but thanked God that, in the end, she had abandoned him. Looking around the town he loved, at the people who meant so much to him, he resolved not to allow anyone, not even Honey Armstrong, sidetrack him.

In his screwed-up mind, she was the two opposing factions in his past—the control and the unrestricted passion.

Even as aware as he was, he didn't know how to see her differently.

She might be good for those two little tykes, but she wasn't the woman for him.

AFTER A BRIEF nap for the children upstairs in Honey's apartment, they ambled down the street toward the park. Honey had an afternoon of grace away from work, since the bar was closed on Mondays.

She was satisfied with today's Rib Fest. They'd raised a lot of money for renovations of the Rodeo fairgrounds.

"We should take the children out to see the rides at the fair," Honey said.

"Yeah," Cole replied. "Maybe. They won't be open for another couple of months, though. Might be disappointing when they can't ride them yet."

"True."

Cole had resisted interviewing more people for the position of nanny only because he was exhausted. As much as he needed everything taken care of, he said, he also needed a day off. Desperately.

Honey understood.

At the playground, a few mothers sat on benches while their children played on the equipment.

They waved to Cole and Honey then watched curiously as they helped the children on the playground apparatus.

Evan ran for the fireman's pole, raced up the ladder and, barely holding on, tossed himself down to land in a heap on the ground.

"Kid's going to kill himself," Cole muttered, picking him up and dusting off his butt. "Be more careful."

Heedless, Evan headed for the slide.

Madeline reached for Cole's hand and pointed to the slide. "You want to go up there?" he asked.

She nodded.

Cole picked her up and set her at the top. She balked and all but jumped back into his arms.

Evan slid down, laughing.

Madeline gestured toward the top again. Cole put her up there and again she jumped back into his arms.

Again and again, Evan slid down while Madeline watched.

"Do you want me to go up with you?" Honey asked.

Madeline nodded and reached for Honey's hand.

Honey took her up the steps and hunched down to get through the covered archway to the top of the slide.

"Good thing I'm small." She laughed.

Expression inscrutable, Cole said, "Yeah."

Honey had no idea what he was thinking. She never had been able to figure him out.

Madeline put her hand on the side of Honey's face to draw her attention back to the task at hand.

"Okay, let's go." Honey put her legs on either side of Madeline's so the child's ankles and knees wouldn't rub against the sides of the slide on the way down. She wrapped her arms around Madeline and pushed off.

"Oh no!" She'd underestimated their combined weights and slid down too fast.

Cole lunged to the bottom of the slide to catch the two of them, lifting Honey by her upper arms and wrapping his own around the two of them so neither hit the ground.

"Good thing you're strong." Honey laughed to cover the confusion sparked in her by the heat and nearness of Cole's body.

She liked him touching her. Really liked it.

His big body set her heart zipping about with hummingbird wings. Crazy.

She put distance between them.

"Did you enjoy the slide?" she murmured in Madeline's ear.

The ghost of a smile tipped up the corners of the child's mouth. "Again," she whispered.

Honey climbed the steps and sat with Madeline between her legs.

Madeline gestured with her tiny fingers for Cole to come back to the bottom of the slide. "Catch."

Cole stood with his legs apart, the denim of his jeans stretching across strong thighs. Solid and dependable and so, so appealing with his arms open, he waited for them.

Yes, Honey thought. *Yes. Wait for us.*

Sunlight caught in his thatch of dirty-blond hair. The breeze mussed it.

Honey had been alone a long time. She'd never minded her independence. She loved it.

But those arms of Cole's…

Waiting for her and Madeline…

He would catch them safely, and that was the problem. His arms felt too good.

Madeline demanded, "Now," and Honey pushed them forward. Again, Cole caught them and lifted into the air, exaggerating the lift for Maddy's sake.

Her smile grew a little and she ordered, "Again."

Honey obliged, again and again, each time both eager for and horrified by Cole's touch. Or rather, horrified by her reaction to it.

She was drooling over the man, for Pete's sake, and craving his touch.

As the two of them stood in Cole's embrace yet again, Madeline whispered, "Make wind again."

Cole's eyes widened. Honey felt her own follow suit.

"It wasn't me," he said.

"I didn't do anything," she responded.

Madeline patted her own cheeks. "Make wind happen on my face again."

Honey started to laugh. She sensed Cole shaking beside her, holding in his laughter. "Oh, *that's* what you mean. You like the wind on your face when we go down the slide fast."

Madeline nodded.

Biting the inside of his cheek, Cole turned aside, but his eyes sparkled.

Honey liked that trace of happiness on his face, the alchemy of a child's unwitting joke transmuting grief to fun.

After a dozen or so times, Cole pretended that hefting them into the air was a chore. Honey knew it was an exaggeration because she could feel his strength and the relative ease with which he lifted them when they hit the bottom.

He huffed and puffed. He moaned.

Madeline laughed.

Cole froze with his arms around both of them. Honey hung in his embrace with her feet off the ground. Cole's stunned deep blue gaze met Honey's. She frowned a question, *what?*

"First time," he whispered.

"Since...?"

"Since." A flat statement, but she knew what he meant. First laughter since the death of her parents.

Honey stared. She'd never been this close to Cole before. How could she never have noticed how expressive his eyes were? How deep blue they were?

Birdsong, the breeze chattering through leaves in the trees, children's laughter in the park... All faded away, her attention distilled to this one moment and this one man.

He let her go slowly, she and Madeline sliding down until her feet hit the ground and she had to ease her head back to look up at him.

He shook his head, one sharp gesture, and frowned. A

second later, his expression flattened and he let her go as though nothing had happened.

As though the earth hadn't shifted on its axis.

Using her best no-nonsense tone, Honey said, "Let's go back to the bar and rustle up supper."

If Cole could pretend nothing had just happened between them, so could she.

Honey and Cole headed back to the apartment with Evan and Madeline. Honey went downstairs to the bar to get out some burgers to feed everyone.

A couple of lights were on. She found Chet sitting in one of the booths with a cup of coffee and an empty plate, reading the various national weekend papers he had delivered from Denver every Monday.

"Don't you spend enough time here?" Honey asked. "You should be reading at home with your feet up in your own living room."

"Quieter here."

Honey understood his point. His wife was a nonstop talker. She enjoyed the company of her friends and her phone conversations. He enjoyed the snatches of quiet time he found here when the bar was closed.

"I'm just getting burgers together for dinner."

Chet stood. "Go on back upstairs. I'll put on a bunch of sliders for the kids. How many burgers for you and Cole?"

"You don't have to—"

"Want to."

"Will you join us for dinner?"

"Just finished leftover ribs and fries. I'll turn the deep fryer back on to make y'all fries."

"Thanks, Chet. You're a gem."

"Aw, go on." His gruff voice elicited a laugh from Honey. Chet liked to think he was a big tough guy, and he could be in the bar, but he was a softie at heart.

"They sleeping upstairs again tonight?" he asked.

Honey huffed out a frustrated laugh. She might love Rodeo, but sometimes living in town was like living in a fishbowl. "Does the whole town know?"

"Yep."

"Yes, they'll stay upstairs one more night, then they'll go to Cole's apartment."

"Bring the children down here for dinner. I like 'em."

"Okay."

Honey gathered everyone downstairs in the bar.

"Maybe Cole can find music you'll like." She took a bunch of quarters out of the cash register and left them in the middle of the booth into which Cole settled the children.

A few minutes later, Patsy Cline sang "Crazy" in the background.

Honey opened a bag of chips and set it on the table, catching the words, "Tomorrow we have to sleep in my apartment."

"Why?" Evan asked.

"Because it will be noisy upstairs. This is a place where people come to listen to loud music, talk and have fun. You won't be able to sleep."

When Evan's attention drifted, Cole brought it back with a finger under his chin. "There's another more important reason why we can't stay. We're inconveniencing Honey greatly. She's used to having her place to herself. We don't want to bother her."

Staring at the two little ones who were burrowing their way into her heart, Honey thought, *Bother me! Please!*

"Do you understand?" Cole asked.

Evan nodded. Clearly Madeline did not have a clue what Cole meant, even if she did take her cue from her older brother and nod when he did.

She took one half of a broken chip between two small fingers and bit it. Evan took a handful and shoved them into his mouth, leaving as many crumbs on his T-shirt as he got in his mouth.

Chet entered the bar with sliders and fries for the children.

Just as he had earlier in the day, he fussed with tying bar towels around their necks as bibs. Like docile little lambs, they let him.

Chet returned to the kitchen, came back with a tray of condiments and doctored their sliders according to their wishes.

"Your burgers will be ready soon, Cole and Honey," he said.

COLE FOLLOWED CHET into the kitchen. "Can I speak to you?"

"What's up?" Chet asked while he threw more fries in for the adults.

"I know it's a huge favor to ask, but can you come in tomorrow morning to babysit for a few minutes?"

"Sure. It's not a huge favor. I like the kids. They're sweet. What's up?"

"I need to find a house for us, but I'm kinda lost. I want Honey to come to the real estate office with me and look everything over."

"Good idea. She's got a good head on her shoulders."

Not that Honey had any more experience than him, but he hoped she might catch something he might miss in what the children would need in a suitable home.

Home. God, what did he know about setting up a home? His parents had given him everything he could ever need financially, but nurturing him? It had never happened.

Now he had to nurture Maddy and Evan. Now he had to not only provide a home, he had to *make* one.

"Cole." Chet's voice pulled him out of his thoughts.

"Yeah?"

"Relax. You're in good hands with Honey."

The children were, at any rate.

He returned to the bar.

Patsy had finished singing and Honey helped Evan to choose another song from the old-fashioned tabletop jukebox.

Madeline picked up a French fry and nibbled on it. Evan bit into his slider. Mustard oozed down his chin. Honey wiped it off with the towel around his neck.

Yes, the children were in good hands.

Back upstairs, the evening's routine was the same as the night before, including Honey waking in the middle of the night to two children crying all over Cole in the living room.

How on earth was he going to make life okay for those two?

She made nests for them on the sofa with Cole, turned the music on low and the single light over the kitchen stove, and left the room after Cole's heartfelt thanks.

THE NEXT MORNING, as they walked along Main Street in the glaring sunlight, Honey asked, "What was it you wanted to show me? Why did Chet have to come in so early to babysit?"

"The real estate office. I need to find a place. Will you advise me?"

"Sure. I'd be happy to." Never in her life had Honey gone house hunting. She'd grown up in her apartment above the bar with her mother. Her parents had owned the building. After her father's death, Honey's mother had seen no reason to get rid of either and had run the bar alone until Honey was old enough to help. Honey had known no other home.

Spending someone else's money, and imagining what might work for those two children, she could totally do.

"It'll be fun," she said.

Cole's look said, *For you, maybe.*

At Julia Hanson's office, they realized—as they should have, had they really thought about it—that there wasn't much available. Rodeo might be a good-size town, but that didn't mean there were a lot of houses for sale.

Julia, a pretty woman with expensive taste in clothes and shoes, took them to one wall displaying photographs of the only sites available. "Cole, I understand your needs, of course," Julia said. "Everyone in town knows about the children. Your apartment is thoroughly unsuitable."

Cole smiled down at her. "You've seen it," he said wryly.

Julia laughed. "A couple of times over the years for each new sheriff. There are only three apartments available in town right now. This one might work."

She pointed to one photo of a long narrow living room, which meant it had to be above a store.

"I don't like the look of it," Cole said, indicating the photo. "It might be larger than my place with the extra bedroom, but it's still dark and narrow. Those kids need…"

He shrugged. "Light. Space. A home. I don't know how to turn any place into a home for them."

Julia rested her fingers on his arm. "I can help you with that, Cole."

And I can break those fingers if you don't let go of Cole. The thought came out of nowhere with a violence as ugly as the words, shocking Honey. She was neither vicious nor jealous.

Come *on.* Cole was just a guy she was helping out. That was all.

A surge of jealousy was not in the cards. Not in her nature. Totally unwarranted.

"Thanks, Julia," Cole said. "I appreciate it. I have Honey's help. She's been great."

Julia removed her fingers and smiled at Honey—maybe a tad falsely?

Whatever. She was keeping her hands to herself, and that was all that mattered.

"I'm thinking I'll have to buy a place," Cole said.

Honey touched one photograph. "The old Asher place is the only one for sale right now, I see. They've been gone for a year."

"It needs work. It isn't move-in ready."

"What needs to be done on it?" Cole asked.

"The structure is sound, but it would need to be cleaned from top to bottom."

"Can you afford cleaning services?" Honey asked Cole.

He nodded. Humph. Again, chatty with Julia, but not with her. And yet, when he'd told Julia he had Honey's help, he'd sounded glad of it, and proud.

Such a confusing man.

They set up a date for Cole to see the place.

"Thanks for your time, Julia. I appreciate it." Cole stepped outside and turned to Honey. "What are your thoughts?"

"The Asher place looks like it could be brought up to date. I grew up in an apartment and was absolutely fine, but you need room for those two children."

They crossed Main and walked toward the bar. "I wasn't traumatized like Evan and Maddy are. I was happy with my mom. You need a house with a yard and with as much hominess as you can pull off."

Cole shook his head like a bewildered little boy. "I don't know how."

Some devil got into her and she placed her fingers on his arm. Startled, he stopped walking and looked down at her.

Honey batted her eyelashes outrageously. "I can help you with that, Cole." She nailed her impression of Julia perfectly.

A slow smile spread across Cole's face. "Catty, Honey."

"Great, huh?"

He laughed and Honey thought the sun might just as well slink away behind the horizon early today, because it sure as hell couldn't compete with the sunshine of Cole's laughter.

They entered the bar, and Cole sobered. Madeline sat on Chet's lap, sobbing quietly. Chet lifted a helpless shoulder.

"Been trying to calm her down since you left. I'm thinkin' maybe you shouldn't have both gone at the same time."

Madeline struggled down from Chet's lap and all but threw herself at Cole. He caught her up in his arms and held her against his chest, murmuring soft, soothing words.

Chet went to the kitchen to make a late breakfast for Cole and Honey. They'd opened the real estate office at nine. It was just shy of ten.

Madeline wouldn't let go of Cole and he couldn't squeeze into the booth with her on his lap, so he sat at a table.

Honey brought over her meal.

From the kitchen, for all the world as though he could see around corners, Chet called, "I'm making her fresh. Don't feed her that. It's cold."

Honey's cell rang. She answered then told Cole, "Rachel's inviting you and the children out to the ranch for lunch and the afternoon. Okay?"

Cole nodded, clearly not knowing what else to do with the children.

Chet entered the room with more food and said, "You go, too, Honey."

"Chet, I have to work this afternoon."

"Come on, Honey. It's Tuesday. Nothing I can't handle."

She opened her mouth to protest, but Madeline suddenly

crawled into her lap and wrapped Honey's hair around her shoulders.

Message received. "Okay, I'll come."

Madeline snuggled against her while she ate a boiled egg. Evan climbed onto Cole's lap.

"Take your time," Chet ordered. "No rushing back here. Got it?"

Honey nodded.

Chapter Seven

They drove out of town to Rachel and Travis's place for the afternoon, taking Cole's truck because he'd bought children's car seats before driving from the airport to Rodeo.

Ten minutes later, they arrived at the Victorian that Travis owned, an anomaly among the ranch houses of the Montana landscape. Travis had come to town last November and bought the big old house Abigail Montgomery had owned until she died.

Rachel had always wanted the house and had been heartbroken that someone else had bought it.

How appropriate that Travis and Rachel had fallen in love. Rachel now lived in her dream home with one of the nicest men Honey had ever met.

Just as they pulled up in the driveway, Travis came out of the house with little Tori by his side. He held her shoulder until the vehicle came to a firm halt then let her come to greet everyone. She tried to open the back door on Madeline's side but couldn't reach.

"Sheriff Cole, hep me. Please. Want to see Maddy."

He stepped out of the truck, his muscled weight moving the heavy vehicle about.

"Why won't you open it?" Tori asked.

Cole laughed. "Because you're standing right in front

of the door. If I open it, I'll knock you over like a bowling pin. Do you want that?"

Tori giggled. "No, Sheriff." A beat later, she asked, "What's a bowling pin?"

A rueful smile kicked up the corner of his mouth. "Never mind. Old-fashioned stuff." He picked her up and set her out of the way. Then he opened the door and lifted Madeline from her car seat.

"Times have changed," Travis said. He'd come up on the other side of the truck to help Evan out of his seat. "Who would have thought a few months ago we'd both have children's car seats and toys filling our pickups?"

They entered Rachel's house.

"Lunch is minestrone, if that's okay with everyone," Rachel asked. "I'm all about easy preparation these days."

"I hear you. Thanks so much for inviting us on short notice."

In the background, Tori chatted away to a silent Madeline. She ran to get a book and shiny star and unicorn stickers. They snuggled next to each other on the sofa and filled pages with stickers.

Throughout lunchtime, Cole and Travis kept up a running commentary about cattle and planting schedules, all of which Honey listened to with half an ear.

She'd heard the same conversation, or variations of it, throughout her years of running the bar.

After lunch, the adults led the children to the barn to visit the animals.

Once inside, Tori stared at Maddy's sandals then threw herself against Cole's leg and said, "Maddy needs cowboy boots."

"Does she?" Cole's eyebrows shot up comically. "I had no idea."

He picked up Madeline by her arms and held her nose to nose. "You want cowboy boots?"

She nodded.

"Then you shall have a pair, my princess."

Madeline hid her face against his shoulder, but Honey saw the tiny smile.

She whispered in his ear.

"You want pink boots like Tori's? Okay."

He settled her onto his forearm. "You want cowboy boots, too, Evan?"

"Yeah."

"Pink?"

"Uncle Co-ole."

He laughed. "Okay. No pink."

They approached one of the horses in the stable.

"This here's Dusty."

Madeline clung to Cole's shoulders and whispered in his ear.

"Yes, he is big, but he's a good boy. He won't hurt you."

"Here." Travis's big hand appeared in front of Cole, holding a carrot. Dusty perked up and tried to snatch it.

Travis jerked it out of his way. "Hold on."

He handed it to Cole.

"Let's hold it together, okay?" Cole said to Madeline.

She wrapped her small fingers around the carrot below Cole's.

"Easy," Travis murmured, and Dusty took it gently, sensing Madeline's fear.

"See?" Cole said. "He's as gentle as a newborn lamb."

Travis laughed. "Not always, but I trust him with the children, as long as there's an adult present."

Madeline whispered in Cole's ear again.

"Yes, he does chew loudly. He needs to improve his table manners."

Again, she hid her face against his shoulder. For the briefest moment, Cole rested his head on her hair, both pain and pleasure flitting across his features.

The moment too intimate, something she felt she should not be witness to, Honey turned away.

Cole did the same with Evan and Honey appreciated his efforts to be fair with both children.

They stepped outside into blazing sunshine.

"Let's have our dessert down by the stream," Rachel said. "I'll go make a couple of thermoses of tea and lemonade. Travis, will you get blankets and fill a basket with the cookies Tori and I made for dessert? Let's bring the grapes and cheese cubes from the fridge, too."

In the kitchen, the children jockeyed for the best view of what went into the baskets.

"You kids can't possibly be hungry," Honey exclaimed. "You just ate."

"But there's cheese, Honey," Evan said. "It's my favorite."

"Is it? I'll make sure to buy some for you and keep it on hand." She talked as though she planned to have them over often after today—absurd. But they'd rapidly blazed a trail straight to her heart. "What kind do you like?"

"Uncle Cole, what kind of cheese do I like?"

He shrugged. "I don't know, Ev, but knowing your mom it was probably something like brie or camembert."

"I know that word *brie*! It's round, right?"

Cole nodded.

"Okay," Honey said. "That's what I'll pick up."

Evan shot her a huge grin and her heart melted yet again.

Every adult carrying a little something, and Rachel bringing up the rear with Beth in her arms, they walked to the stream—not, as it turned out, a short walk.

Brilliant, Honey thought. *Rachel knows how to wear out children.*

The kids threw stones and trailed twigs and small branches in the water. Cole and Travis watched to make sure no one fell in. It might be the end of June, but there was still a breeze and it was too cool for the children to get wet, despite the beauty of the day.

In the shade, Rachel sat with Beth, who watched the children's antics.

Honey joined the kids at the stream, naming the leaves of different trees as they floated by.

Evan raced to and fro for more stones to toss into the stream.

"You keep doing that," Cole said, "and you'll build a dam. The stream won't be able to keep flowing."

Evan laughed. Honey grasped his hands and spun him around.

Then everything turned into a slow-motion movie reel as Honey stepped too close to the edge and the ground gave out beneath her feet.

Travis lunged and caught Evan before he hit the water.

Cole rushed to catch Honey.

He lost his footing on muddy ground, slipped and they both landed in the stream, Honey on top of Cole.

Cole said, "Oof!" and Honey squealed, "Cold!"

Cole stood, taking Honey with him. "Water's definitely still cold."

On the bank, Honey shivered, even with Cole's arms still wrapped around her.

He carried her to the grass beside the picnic blankets. The two stood dripping on dry ground.

Honey caught Cole staring at her. She glanced down at herself. Her pink cotton blouse clung to her, turned see-through by the water, showing her white lace demi-bra in detail.

"Honey," Tori squealed. "I can see your underwear top. It's prettier than Mommy's."

Rachel laughed and tossed Honey a dish towel from one of the baskets. "Cover up with this."

Honey tucked it into the front of the blouse's neckline and felt better.

Not one to flaunt her body, her clothes were pretty but not alluring. Apparently, that all changed once they got wet. Vy said her feminine clothing contrasted with her take-charge personality. Honey didn't think about it much, but she wondered if that was part of the appeal of pretty clothes. They contrasted her job and the no-nonsense way in which she had to handle sometimes rowdy customers.

Cole sat on the blanket and the children sat near him. In time, Evan fell asleep and Madeline's lids drooped.

Honey wrung water from her skirt.

Rachel quietly packed the baskets. "Why don't you and Cole stay here with the children? Don't disturb them. They're exhausted and need their sleep, but this is a longer picnic than I'd planned and I need to put Beth down for her nap and do some laundry."

"That's fine, Rachel. We'll head home after the kids wake up. Thanks for having us over."

"Here, Honey," Tori said. "Take this home for Maddy and Evan. They like unicorns."

She handed Honey the sticker book.

Travis packed the cards and toys they'd brought. He shook out the blanket that was no longer occupied and carried it over to Honey.

Quietly, he said, "Wrap this around yourself."

Rachel cleared the baskets from the other blanket and Travis covered Evan and now sleeping Madeline with it. Cole tucked it all around them.

Rachel, Travis and Tori left Cole and Honey sitting on the blanket bookending the sleeping children.

They sat quietly with nothing to say.

A chain of ants walked across the farthest corner of the blanket.

A bird whistled in a branch above Honey's head.

The breeze ruffled still-new green leaves of the tree above them, mild but cool wherever Honey's clothing was still wet.

She curled forward and leaned her head onto her knees to keep her body heat contained.

Eventually, she nodded off.

She awoke slowly, by increments, not wanting to stir because she felt so good. Warm. Safe.

She burrowed against the source of the heat, wrapping her arms around it. A voice murmured nearby, rumbling against her cheek.

A hand brushed across her hair.

What?

Her eyes sprang open. She came fully awake to find herself nestled onto Cole's lap, in his arms.

Pushing against the chest she'd been leaning on, she stared at him.

This close, his eyes dark in the shade, almost navy, he looked less intimidating. Warmer.

She sat across his lap with her legs drawn up to her chest. His arms circled her and his knees at her back protected her from the breeze.

"You were shivering," he said, again with that voice that rumbled through her.

She stared.

"I couldn't leave you cold."

He started to lift her from his lap. Too soon. She held on.

"Are you still cold?" he asked.

"Yes."

He didn't seem upset about having to hold her to keep her warm. His big hand reached for the back of her head and urged her back against his chest.

"Breeze is a little cool." He sounded perfectly normal, as though he did this every day. As though it was normal for him to offer a woman warmth by holding her on his lap and wrapping hard, truly comforting arms around her.

Honey hadn't felt so…so…*taken care of* in ages. In years.

She relaxed against him, the more to enjoy this rare event, the likes of which probably wouldn't happen again for years.

She led an active and full life…during opening hours, that is.

This summer would be brutally busy until August, when she and the other organizers would put on the first reincarnation of the fair and rodeo in fifteen years. After that, her free time would be hers again. Maybe too much free time. Wrapped in Cole's arms, she could acknowledge to herself that sometimes she got lonely.

Cole smelled good, like soap and fresh air and heat.

The hair on his forearm beneath her hand abraded her palm, but softly. She rubbed it, slowly moving her hand along his arm, shaping her fingers around the long muscles.

She couldn't see his hand where it curled around her calf, but behind her closed eyelids, she could imagine it. She knew it was a strong square hand. The rare times that he had to fight in her bar, she knew he made a strong square fist.

Funny. Why had she noticed that detail and why would she remember it?

Her hand, with a mind of its own, eased up to his bicep, where it cradled the full, magnificent strength of him.

His chest rose and fell, the motion taking her head with it. The pulse beneath her ear quickened and began to pound.

The muscles in his thighs beneath her tensed.

Her fingers caressed his bicep through the fabric of his denim shirt. She wished it were bare, like his forearms, where the cuffs of his sleeves were rolled back, the skin there so warm.

How warm would it be closer to his source, his heart? If she could touch his naked chest—

"Honey?"

His voice startled her out of her *thoroughly* inappropriate thoughts of the town sheriff.

"Yes?" She held her breath.

"Maybe you should stop touching me."

To her horror, she realized her hand had indeed moved to his chest. Her forefinger had slipped into the open vee of his shirt, where the skin really was warmer.

The world spun when he set her on the blanket, surged to his feet and stalked to the edge of the stream.

Honey straightened herself. "I'm so sorry. I don't know what came over me." Her voice squeaked out of her on a weak breath. So unlike her.

"Just..." He cleared his throat. "Just perfectly normal attraction between a man and a woman. That's all."

Evan sat up, breaking the tension between them. "Where is everyone?" He rubbed his eyes.

Cole came back to the blanket. He looked like himself again, in control. Calm.

Honey, often the master of control, still had a drumming pulse and a racing heart.

Madeline came awake. Cole picked her up and said, "We'd better head back."

Honey busied herself with folding blankets and making sure they had everything, but her hands shook.

How thoroughly embarrassing. She *never* lost control.

Evan ran ahead, Cole carrying Madeline and walking with long strides, as though he couldn't wait to get away from Honey. And why not?

Pulling up the rear, Honey berated herself for her behavior. Cole needed help with the children. He didn't need a woman coming on to him just because he had generously offered his body for warmth.

She trudged behind them, wondering what on earth had come over her.

Men made passes at Honey all the time. She knew she was an attractive woman. But she didn't let it go to her head. As a businesswoman, in particular as a bar owner, she protected her reputation.

Would Cole brag to the men in town that Honey Armstrong had come on to him?

She studied Cole's strong, straight back.

The answer hit her with resounding confidence. No. Cole would never do that.

She knew in her bones that he was an honorable man.

Cole Payette was a gentleman through and through.

COLE WISHED HE hadn't been raised as a gentleman, with old-fashioned values like honor and decency, and respect for women.

What he really wanted to do was to find a babysitter, drop off the children and drag Honey to her lacy bedroom, where he would spend hours worshipping her perfect body.

His hands shook with his need.

On the long walk back to the truck, while he buckled the children into their seats and while he drove back to Honey's Place, his hands shook with a fine tremor that seemed to run through every inch of his body.

He wondered if it showed.

He hoped not.

A man who prided himself on his self-control, Cole had been brought to the edge this afternoon by Honey.

His impulse to hold her, to warm her, had been pure. She'd been shivering in her sleep. He had felt the chill of being wet in the June breeze.

So small compared to him, her body would have been far colder.

She hadn't awakened when he'd picked her up and settled her onto his lap. She'd snoozed while he wrapped his arms and thighs up around her to keep her warm, secretly enjoying a few moments of forbidden pleasure just holding her.

Then she'd come out of her doze and had wreaked havoc with his equilibrium.

That one wandering hand, so small but so lethal, had aroused him beyond bearing.

He wondered that she hadn't run screaming from him when she'd realized. He'd always been careful that his attraction to her didn't show and that he didn't touch her.

This was why.

He wanted her.

Horrified that his two children slept a foot away while he dreamed about doing everything he'd ever wanted to do with Honey, he'd dropped her like a burning coal and had stalked to the stream.

If it could have helped, he would have walked straight into the cool soothing water.

Used to being in control, he'd brought himself in line so he could get all of them home, but still he thought about that hand on his body, and that one finger tucked against the bare skin of his chest.

Honey Armstrong exerted a powerful force over him.

She'd brought her fall into the stream on herself by dancing with Evan. She should have known the edge of the stream might not be secure.

Or was he being overly critical? Was he trying to find fault with her for the sake of his equilibrium?

Back in her apartment, he said, "Can you watch the children for a few minutes? I need to change." The seams of his denim jeans were still damp and uncomfortable.

Honey nodded. "I'll call Chet and tell him we're home. He'll make us supper downstairs."

"Okay." Cole practically ran out of the apartment.

Honey still had that ridiculous tea towel tucked into her blouse. Even so, she looked like an angel. Her hair had dried to a curly halo.

As he strode across the road to his apartment, one image shimmered in his memory: Honey's pale pink blouse plastered to her body, showing her bra holding breasts that were about as perfect as anything Cole had ever seen in his life.

Somehow, *somehow* he had to get past his attraction to her. He had two children to take care of, both of whom had grown attached to Honey already. He couldn't just walk away from her.

He wouldn't be able to avoid Honey.

For the first time since coming home to Rodeo after the funeral, he cursed his impulse to go to Honey for help.

Until today, he'd not questioned why. There were dozens of caring people in Rodeo who would have stepped up to help.

But he had wanted Honey. For the entire trip home after the funeral, drowning in grief with two children who were suddenly his, and with his world shattered, one thought had run through his mind: if he could only get home to Honey, all would be well.

Look how that was turning out.

Yes, he was home with Honey. Yes, Madeline and Evan responded to her.

But so did Cole—too much—with all of his wild, crazy longings for her pushing him to do things they'd both regret.

At that moment, he liked her take-charge attitude that helped him to cope with this new life. He even liked how the children responded to the childlike, whimsical, too fun-loving carefree side that bothered him so much and reminded him too much of Shiloh.

Cole, you are one sick guy.

With the force of his will, he built the walls around his heart that he needed to get through the near future…and beyond. For the rest of his life in Rodeo.

THE FOLLOWING MORNING, Honey said, "You have to contact Maria Tripoli. You know you won't find anyone more perfect in Rodeo."

Cole sighed. "Yeah. I know. I'll call her today."

"The children can stay here until about three when I go down to the bar, then you need to get them back to your place and used to spending time with Maria. Maybe you and Maria can take them to the playground again. They liked it there."

Cole nodded with resignation.

"It will be noisy tonight. Even if it is only Wednesday night, the children won't be used to that level of noise. You'll have to make do at your apartment."

"I will, Honey. We'll be out of your hair tonight."

As he passed her to go to the kitchen, she snagged him. "Cole, stop. You aren't *in my hair*. I'm thinking of what's best for the children."

Evan said, "I want to keep staying here."

Madeline had twisted around on the kitchen chair and stared at Honey through the rungs, her expression a picture of absolute betrayal and reproach.

Oh, darling, don't look at me like that.

"Let's face this all later," she whispered to Cole. "We can still have fun today."

"Yes." He picked up Madeline.

Honey smiled for her sake. "Let's go to the diner for breakfast. It's fun there."

Of the child in his arms Cole asked, "Madeline, do you want to go out for pancakes?"

"I'm Maddy," she whispered.

Cole's eyebrows rose, but then he smiled. To Honey, he said, "That's a really nice idea. Let's do it."

Before they left, he called Maria and set up the afternoon. Honey wished he didn't look so unhappy about it.

At the diner, they found a rare empty booth in the window. Evan slid in to sit beside the window, Maddy followed and Cole moved to sit on the other side with Honey, but Maddy made a sound of distress.

He changed direction and sat beside her. She settled.

They ate pancakes and then left the diner, intent on filling in time until Maria arrived.

They walked slowly, because all that waited for them at Honey's was an empty apartment.

"I need to find things for them to do," Honey said.

Cole chewed on his lower lip. "They have only a few of their favorite toys and books here."

"What about the other toys they owned? What happened to their parents' things?"

"I took only what I could carry on the plane with the two little ones. I sorted the rest and packed up the stuff I thought should be keepsakes for them. It's being shipped here."

He frowned. "I guess I should buy games? What kinds of games? And anything else?"

"We should have asked Rachel."

"Yeah. Do you want to call her?"

Honey got out her cell phone. When she asked her question, Rachel turned out to be a font of information, of course.

"Pick up children's playing cards. Go Fish, especially. Coloring books. Craft supplies. Large, sturdy jigsaw puzzles. Lego."

Honey relayed all of the information to Cole.

"I'll go to the toy store at the mall and see what they have."

"Video games!" Evan shouted.

Rachel must have heard him, because she said, "Don't start them early on that kind of thing. Keep their hands and minds busy. Keep them active."

Honey thanked Rachel and hung up. They continued their walk down Main.

Beside her, Cole came to an abrupt halt. His sudden rigidity puzzled Honey. She followed his gaze across the street to a couple standing in front of the cop shop, being given directions by one of Cole's deputies.

Spotting Cole, Deputy Mortimer became animated, as though saying, "There he is."

The older couple he spoke to followed his pointing finger and watched Cole, expressions carefully neutral.

Even so, Honey picked up a subtle disapproval.

Of Cole? How could that be? *Everyone* loved Cole.

Uptight and old-fashioned in their conservative clothing, they started across the street toward Cole.

Tension arced from him like sheet lightning. An urge arose in Honey to take his hand, to console and, strangely, to protect him from the ill will radiating from those two people.

As they came closer, she realized they weren't as old as they seemed, possibly mid-sixties, but they gave the impression of being from an even older generation.

Odd. Most people wanted to look younger, not older.

Honey sidled close to Cole and asked, "Who are they?"

Cole, not happy at all, said, "My parents."

Chapter Eight

Rage blinded Cole.

They'd come here. To Rodeo, Montana.

To his safe haven.

His place.

He'd told them, had *ordered* them not to come to town. But when had they ever respected his wishes?

Rampaging memories engulfed him, of his mother and grandmother, lecturing. Always lecturing.

He was six years old and wondering why he couldn't play with the other children.

He was nine and resisting his exalted standing in the community.

He was twelve and hemmed in on all sides by his mother's ambition.

He was sixteen and rushing home after school wondering why the other members of the football team were *riffraff.*

He was eighteen and chafing against the pressure of an advantageous relationship with his mother's friend's daughter.

He was twenty and fighting against his parents' choice of college and career and wife for him.

He was twenty-one and running away with Shiloh, the antithesis of his mother.

His hemmed-in and controlled life, from which his sister had also escaped, had never been more than a memory away.

Now, here it came racing back in the flesh.

When Frank and Ada Payette reached his side of the street, Cole went on the offensive. "The will was final and clear."

He wasted no time on civilities.

No *hello*.

No *why have you come*.

He already knew why they were here.

"It isn't right," his mother said, lipstick bleeding into small lines radiating from tight lips. "You're a single man."

"Last time I checked, yes."

"Show your mother respect," his father barked.

Maddy cried, and Cole lifted her into his arms. Evan sidled against Cole, wrapping his arm around his leg and leaving not an iota of space between them.

"This is helping how?" Cole asked his parents.

"If you would just give the children to us to raise, there wouldn't be all of this tension."

"If you would stay home and leave the raising of them to me," Cole countered, "there wouldn't be this tension."

He stepped around the couple and said, "Come on, Honey. Let's take Evan and Maddy home."

Damn. That hadn't sounded the way Cole had meant it to. It sounded like he and Honey were living together. While that might have figured in a few of his daydreams, it wasn't anywhere close to true, or even possible considering his resistance to her.

"And where exactly is home?" his father asked as they fell in behind him on their journey toward the end of the street.

"My home is an apartment above the sheriff's office, as I'm sure my deputy already informed you."

Cole kept walking forward, hoping he could lose them as he might a curious cat following him home.

No such luck, of course.

"So why are we walking toward some other home, as you just mentioned?" his father asked.

"I'm taking them to a temporary home while I find a larger place for us."

"Are they staying with your girlfriend here? Your *honey*?"

Honey stopped and confronted him. "My name is Honey Armstrong. It is neither a nickname nor an endearment."

It had figured in many of Cole's more graphic dreams as an endearment.

"It is my given name," she continued. "Use it with respect or don't use it at all. I am not Cole's girlfriend and never have been. We are a close-knit community in this town. We help out our neighbors. I'm helping Cole because I have the space for these children that he doesn't have at the moment."

She stopped to open the door to the staircase that led to her apartment.

When his parents noticed it was above a bar, his mother gasped. It gave Cole no small amount of satisfaction.

"You live *here*? Above a bar?"

"Yes," Honey replied. "I own the bar."

His mother shot him a scathing look. "You are entrusting the care of Alexandra's children to a *bar* owner?"

"Alexandra and *Dennis's* children. Don't forget about Dennis, as you were wont to do when he was alive, poor guy. Sandy told me all about your treatment of him."

He felt Honey staring at him. The change in his language, he guessed. When he was with his parents, it became more formal and harked back to another time. Another life.

"Sandy chose Dennis as her husband because she loved him. He was a good man."

"Her name was Alexandra." His mother used what he called her forceful voice. She didn't raise it and yet, it came out stronger.

"*Sandy* wouldn't allow you to control her choice of husband as you did every other aspect of her life while she was growing up."

"I did what was best for both of you."

"No. You did what was best for *you*. Against all odds, Sandy and I had enough backbone to get out from under your thumb. We wanted our own lives. To make our own choices, not yours." He gestured around Main Street. "This town has been good to me. And *for* me."

He liked it here in Rodeo. If he had his way, he'd never have another thing to do with his past. But here it was in the form of his overbearing mom and his spineless dad who would do anything his mother and her mother ordered.

No wonder Cole had had his fill of controlling women. No wonder he'd run off with Shiloh.

His reactions as an adult made perfect sense considering where he'd come from.

He'd chosen not to be a carbon copy of his father who had moved onto the Ducharme family estate upon marrying Ada. Frank might not have minded being under the matriarch's thumb, but Cole had gotten out of his grandmother's house just in time. He hadn't returned for her funeral.

Another strike against him.

He refused to be molded in the way his father had.

He would be damned if he let his mother kill Evan's and Madeline's spirits as she had tried to do with him and his sister.

"*Both* Dennis and Sandy gave the children into my care," he said. "They trusted me enough to do that."

"We'll see what a judge thinks when he finds out they are living with a bar owner above a bar."

"What do you mean?"

"Since you've been unreasonable about this," his father said, "we've hired an attorney to get custody."

"*Unreasonable?* What's unreasonable about following Sandy's wishes?"

"We have more to offer the children."

"Financially. That's it. There isn't one ounce of warmth or motherly instinct in you."

"Nevertheless," his father cut in, "we have the financial advantage. Any judge in the country, even in this county, will see it our way."

"Especially given where these poor children are being forced to live."

At that moment, Cole hated his mother. He'd always disliked her. He'd always been angry. But he'd never hated her. Now he did.

All the satisfaction he'd taken in Sandy and Dennis's airtight will evaporated from him like a cool mist on a hot day, leaving him parched and scared.

Could they take the kids?

When he gazed down at his children, dread settled in his chest.

Evan clung ever closer to his leg.

Madeline tried to burrow into Cole's chest.

Aware of listening ears, he couldn't deliver the stinging rebuke his parents deserved, but he could make clear to them in no uncertain terms that Maddy and Evan were his and always would be.

If they wanted a fight, he would fight tooth and nail.

"You're welcome to have a role in their lives, but you can't have them. Show your daughter's memory the respect she deserved in life. She wanted them with me. Here is where they will stay."

He turned away to usher them indoors.

"Didn't you hear me?" His mother raised her voice. "In this, we will win."

Why was it so important for her to raise two young children? Because she'd lost control of him and Sandy? So what? That had been fourteen years ago.

"Why do you still need control? Why take Sandy's children? What can they possibly mean to you?"

"They deserve to be raised in the manner to which they should have been born. We can give them everything. They can go to the right schools. Choose the right careers. Take their place in society."

Now they were getting down to the heart of the matter. The Ducharme family was Georgia's version of royalty, and revered for miles around. They could trace their family tree back to pre-Revolutionary France. They had produced most of the lawyers and judges who ran the district in which Cole grew up.

Upon graduation, he had been slated to enter the law firm founded by his great-grandfather. Instead, he'd run away with Shiloh and now served in a different branch of the law.

With Sandy now dead, and Cole out of reach, and with no cousins left, their family influence was over. His choice to leave had been a death knell for the Ducharme family of Georgia.

Was that the reason his mother looked almost desperate?

"I get it," he said. "You didn't get your dynasty out of Sandy and me, so you want to do it through her children."

His mother's knuckles turned white on the strap of her handbag. He'd hit the nail on the head.

He set Madeline down beside her brother and leaned close so the children wouldn't hear. "I knew you didn't want them because you loved them."

Her face twitched, the merest suggestion that it had been

a direct hit. Was she even capable of love? He'd stopped believing so years ago. He hated to think so badly of his parents, but the evidence in his life, during his vulnerable formative years, had been indisputable.

Never in the past had he thought of them as evil. This behavior? Coming here like this? Working directly against Sandy's wishes and trying to steal the children from him?

Yeah, he would call that evil.

"We've hired a lawyer," his mother repeated. "We will get custody."

Over Cole's dead body.

"You can try," Cole said before entering Honey's stairwell and closing the door behind the four of them, blocking out the sight of his parents, but also the sunlight and warmth of what had been a glorious day.

At the top of the stairs, Honey set up the children in their cave with the sticker book Tori had given them yesterday.

"Call Maria and tell her I'll need her here by two thirty at the latest," Honey said. "Go get toys for the children. Then get on with your life as usual. Forget about *them*."

He should object to her bossing him around. It was exactly the kind of behavior his mother pulled, but at the moment it served its purpose.

He straightened his spine. "You're right. I'll be back soon."

He turned and left.

Forty-five minutes later, he returned with all of the kinds of toys Rachel had recommended. When he dropped the bags on the floor in the middle of Honey's carpet, Evan and Madeline riffled through them.

Their joy and appreciation lifted Cole's spirits.

Honey smiled at him and gave him a thumbs-up.

Her optimism boosted him further.

He smiled.

His parents would never get control of Sandy's children.

MARIA TRIPOLI ARRIVED at two thirty on the dot.

"Thanks so much for coming," Cole said.

"You know I'm happy to be here. Children, do you remember me? We met the other day. Call me Maria."

Evan nodded, but Madeline turned away and hid her face in a pillow.

Sorry, Honey mouthed.

Maria shook her head. "We will be fine. Go to work and don't worry about a thing. Cole will help us to become acquainted."

"Let me get changed." In her bedroom, Honey took off the blouse that was covered with smears and splotches of ketchup from the grilled cheese sandwiches she'd made for lunch.

Madeline had sat on her lap. Evan had touched her often. Honey was left to realize how much the children needed to touch and to be held.

They were becoming comfortable with her and liked to hug her, even when their hands weren't as clean as they should be. A small price to pay, in Honey's estimation, for their comfort.

When ready, she slipped into the living room.

"Cole, try to get the children into bed by eight for a good night's sleep." She gave both Evan and Maddy kisses. "Also, Maria, could you share with Cole whatever motherly advice you have?"

Maria laughed. "I have plenty of that. Free of charge."

Honey left knowing the children were in good hands.

She rushed through dinner service. On Wednesday evenings, the crowd wasn't too large, so only she and Chet worked.

She didn't have time to think much about Evan and

Madeline until it slowed down later in the evening and patrons came in for a beer or two and not much food.

Only then did her thoughts wander to Cole and the children, wondering how they were doing.

She checked her watch. Nine o'clock already.

So they wouldn't be upstairs. Cole would have taken them to his apartment. Maria would have gone home hours ago. How had the children reacted to her?

Funny that after only three days Honey missed the thought of them in her apartment. Strange to think of going upstairs later tonight and finding it empty.

Curiously, she would miss not only the children but Cole, too.

Honey cleaned dirty glasses at the bar while Chet read the local paper at a booth.

Chet spoke up so everyone could hear. "Nadine wrote a great article about the fair and rodeo."

Honey and the few drinkers still in the bar listened while he read it aloud.

"Good." Honey stacked clean towels. "We need exposure. We have to do something to bring money back to town, Chet."

"Yeah, and keep the kids here, too, by providing jobs. It'll work, Honey. Y'all are doin' a fine thing for the town."

Local retiree Lester Voile wandered in and sat at the bar. Honey pulled him a draft and set it on a coaster in front of him.

"What was on the menu at the diner tonight?" she asked.

"Meat loaf and garlic mashed potatoes," he said. "My favorite. Will did this thing with cauliflower. Rolled it in cornmeal and cinnamon and roasted it."

"Any good?"

"Delish."

Lester didn't cook, but he watched the Food Network and constantly brought Vy and Will ideas for new dishes.

Clint and Jamie Enright came in, brothers from different mothers. They were good friends, but sometimes they fought when they got drunk. Wednesdays might be slow, but Honey's Place still had its regulars.

"You boys be good tonight," Honey said, pulling drafts. "No fighting."

"Heard the sheriff has his hands full with a couple of kids. Sad, eh?"

Clint wiped foam from his mustache. A second later, Jamie did the same.

Honey's phone rang. She leaned against the counter to answer it. Probably Rachel after putting the children to bed and wanting to chat.

"Have you seen Madeline?"

She straightened abruptly. "Cole?" She barely recognized his panic-stricken voice. "What's happening?"

Alerted by Honey's tone, everyone in the bar stopped talking to listen in.

"I put the children to bed at eight like you said and just went to see if they were sleeping."

"And?"

"And Evan's out like a light, but Madeline's not in her bed. Or in the apartment."

Honey's pulse backed up in her throat. Not in the apartment. Outside? Alone? "You're sure? You've checked everywhere?"

"Of course!" he yelled.

"Okay. Okay." Honey bit her thumbnail.

"I got the deputies out searching."

"I can help you search. Where do you think she would go?"

"Hell, I don't know."

"I'll be right there."

Cole hung up.

"Chet?" Honey said.

He was already heaving himself out of the booth. "What's up?"

"Madeline's missing."

"*Missing?* Jeez. Seriously?"

"I'm going to go look for her. You need to come to stay with Evan so Cole can get out to search."

"What about the bar?" He untied his apron and tossed it onto a table.

Jamie and Clint both stood up. "We got this. Go."

Honey rushed out onto Main Street, Chet hot on her heels. A local rancher slowed his truck to let them run across the road.

She pushed open Cole's unlocked front door and took the steps up to his apartment two at a time. Big Chet came along behind her more slowly. Without knocking, she burst through the door at the top of the stairs.

"Cole?"

He stepped out from the hallway that led to the bedroom. "Here."

After one look at his ravaged face, Honey rushed against him and wrapped her arms around his waist.

"We'll find her," she whispered, terrified it might not be true.

She felt his hands on her back, in her hair.

"I'm scared." A huge admission from Cole.

Honey had seen him handle pretty well every emergency the town and the elements had ever thrown at him. The guy was unflappable.

At the moment, he shook. Thank goodness he was wise enough to ask for help.

Honey forced conviction into her voice. "I said we'll find her and we will, Cole."

He laughed, but roughly. "I knew I could depend on you to make me feel better. Does nothing ever ruffle you, Honey Armstrong?"

The children and their needs.
Madeline's disappearance.
You, lately.

On that final admission to herself, she stepped away from him. "How long do you think Madeline's been gone?"

"At a guess, half an hour. She couldn't have slipped past while I was reading on the sofa."

"What happened? Did you fall asleep?" As exhausted as he was, no one would blame him.

"No. I had to use the washroom."

"Is she so sneaky that she would wait for you to be indisposed?"

"I wouldn't have thought so, but I guess I was wrong."

"Dear God." Honey rubbed her temples. "Where could she have gone?"

Cole closed his eyes and shoved his fingers through his hair, leaving it in unruly rills. "I don't know."

He looked past her toward Chet.

"You two go," Chet said. "Check where you think she might be. I'll stay here in case Evan wakes up."

"Is he still asleep?" Honey asked.

"I just checked on him," Cole said. "Out like a light."

"Okay. Go." Chet shooed them out the door.

Downstairs on the street, Cole said, "I'm going to check the park. She loved the slide. Remember?"

How could she forget? She'd loved it, too, sliding into Cole's strong arms time and again.

"Could she have gone there?"

Cole glanced at the darkening sky. "God, I hope she's not in that park alone."

After Cole left, Honey paced on the pavement, thinking. Thinking.

Lester Voile left the bar across the street and waved to her. "Gonna check the streets."

"Thanks, Lester." The people in this town were so great.

She knew she could trust Jamie and Clint to handle customers and take payment for drinks. They'd close down if they had to. She had all night to find Madeline before heading up to her...empty...apartment...

Madeline!

She hadn't wanted to sleep in Cole's apartment. Had the child decided to go to Honey's place on her own?

Honey raced back across the street and up her stairs to burst into her apartment, breathless with exertion and anxiety.

She turned on a small lamp on a table just inside the door.

Madeline had liked all of Honey's lace and her big pillows. Thinking the child might have wanted to sleep in Honey's bed, she ran to her bedroom.

Empty. The bed, untouched by even the smallest depression to suggest the child might have been there at some point, left Honey as hollow as the room.

Her adrenaline deflated. She'd felt so sure...

She swore. She wasn't much for profanity—she heard too much of it in the bar—but her terror for Madeline's safety left her shaken.

In the living room, she went to the window to look out. Cole stalked down the street. Madeline wasn't in the park.

But if not there, *where*?

On the far end of the town ran a small stream. Maddy couldn't be exploring that, could she? What if she'd fallen in? What if the child was already dead?

She had to tell Cole to check there.

She spun around to go to him, only to pull up short.

There, in the armchair and afghan cave, one tiny foot stuck out—Madeline, sound asleep under an afghan.

Honey's legs gave out. She fell onto the desk chair and buried her head in her hands.

Oh, thank God. Oh, sweet freaking Jesus, thank you.
Madeline was safe.

Cole would be frantic.

Honey grabbed the phone and scooted down the hallway to her bedroom, closing the door behind her.

He answered his cell on the first ring.

"She's here," Honey blurted.

"Thank God!" Cole's voice thundered out of him. "She went back home? But where did she go? Did she say?"

"No. Sorry. By *here*, I mean in my apartment."

"Where she wanted to stay earlier."

"Where she wanted to stay," Honey confirmed, "but we wouldn't let her."

"I'm here."

When she heard his footsteps on her stairs, Honey hung up.

Cole came through the door like an avenging archangel, big and dynamic. She pressed a finger to her lips, stepped into the living room and pointed to the cave.

He tiptoed around to the front and squatted down. Gently, he pulled the afghan over the child's bare foot.

He buried his face in his hands and breathed hard. He trembled with the effort to control his emotions.

When he stood, his eyes glistened in the yellow glow of the lamplight.

"What now?" he asked.

"I'll keep her here."

"What about the bar?"

"The Enright brothers are down there right now. Chet can come back from your place and take over. He'll only run into trouble if he needs to cook and serve drinks at the same time."

"I'll get Evan and bring him over here. He'll be upset if he wakes and finds Maddy gone." He scrubbed his hands over his eyes. "God, I'm sorry, Honey. I've been nothing but a pain for you since I returned to town."

"Not true," she responded quietly.

He stared, hair dirty gold in the warm yellow lamp-light. Eyes in shadow, but his actions intent, he took a step toward her. Maybe she'd let too much emotion leak into her voice.

She held her breath.

Madeline woke up crying. Cole pulled up short. Honey wouldn't find out what he'd planned to say. Instead, he picked up the child.

"Hey, hey, shush."

Madeline curled against him with her thumb in her mouth.

"Why did you run away?"

"Want Honey." Madeline hiccuped. "Get Honey."

"She's here now."

Madeline's head popped up. When she saw Honey, she stretched her arms toward her.

Honey took her and clasped her to her chest. "It's okay. I'm here."

Cole smoothed his hand over the child's hair.

"I'm going to bring Evan over and we'll sleep here again tonight."

"Okay," Madeline answered. Honey smiled.

Cole left and returned moments later with Evan half-asleep in his arms. He put him in the spare bedroom.

When he tried to take Madeline from Honey to put her there, too, she resisted, her little arms and legs grasping Honey with surprising strength. "No. Stay with Honey."

"You are staying here, but Honey has to go downstairs to her job at the bar."

"No," Madeline wailed, breaking into wrenching sobs.

Honey stared at Cole.

He said, "I'm sorry."

She shook her head. "She's still so close to what happened. She isn't being a brat. She's missing her parents. Her mother. She's hurting."

"I don't know what's right, Honey."

"Chet can close up tonight."

He blew out a breath. "I'll go run the bar so Chet can cook. I've done it often enough. That okay with you?"

Honey patted Madeline's back. "Yes."

"If there's no one around, or if no one minds, I'll close early."

"Might as well. Knowing what's going on, no one will mind. There weren't many customers when I left." She nodded toward the door at the end of the hallway. "When you're done for the night, come up those stairs."

"I'll lock the street door when I go out."

"Thanks."

After Cole left, Honey put Madeline into bed beside her brother and sat on the side of the bed, smoothing her hair until she fell asleep.

She sat in her living room but couldn't settle down. The latest novel she'd picked up didn't appeal. There was nothing on TV worth watching. She wasn't even satisfied with her computer games tonight.

This all felt too strange.

Compassion overrode any anger or frustration she felt, but even so, she should be down in her bar.

At midnight, she gave up trying to entertain herself, made up Cole's bed on the sofa and headed to her own bed.

An hour later, she woke up with a child on either side of her, fast asleep. They must miss their parents so much.

Giving in to the inevitable, she tucked the covers around them, nestled their heads under her arms and surrendered to exhaustion.

Chapter Nine

Shortly after one in the morning, Cole trudged up the back staircase to Honey's apartment, rubbing the back of his neck where he carried his tension. He planned to wash up and make up a bed on the sofa as quietly as possible.

Passing Honey's bedroom, he noted the open door.

He should close it in case the kids woke up.

Reaching for the doorknob to pull it shut, he halted.

Faint moonlight streaming through a gap in the curtains fell on her bed.

She wasn't alone.

Madeline curled between Honey on one side and the wall on the other. Her head rested on Honey's outstretched arm. Crooked against the wall, Honey's wrist looked uncomfortable.

On Honey's right side, Evan sprawled, taking up an unfair share of the bed.

Cole stepped close. Honey lay on her back, her hair spread around her head in glorious disarray. He understood Madeline's fascination with it. He'd spent endless hours sitting on a bar stool fantasizing about running his fingers through it.

In her sleep, she looked younger than her twenty-eight years. Always happy, always laughing with her customers, she'd taken on a lot of responsibility, too, in running her business alone since her mother's death.

Asleep, the worry lines that sometimes made a show disappeared, leaving only peace.

He'd often wondered if, as much as she loved Honey's Place and liked to run things, it ever felt like a burden.

With the children, he'd added to her burdens.

Shame on him.

Reaching for Evan, he picked up the boy to take him back to his own bed.

Honey stirred and opened her eyes.

Disoriented, her gaze cast about until she saw him and realized what was happening.

"He can stay."

"No. I'll put him to bed."

"Leave Madeline, though. I don't want her upset again."

"Okay."

Cole in Honey's bedroom. Honey in bed amid a froth of lace. Two children. One in Honey's arms and one in Cole's.

A family. Like the dream he'd always had about Honey, while she'd barely been aware of him as a man.

A spear of longing so sharp his eyes watered stabbed through Cole. He hadn't realized how much resisting making advances toward Honey had cost him all of these years.

He rushed from the room.

Had he been in there without the children, had there been only Honey in her amazing, beautiful glory in her inviting bed, he might have begged her to let him stay.

He felt her gaze follow him out of the room.

In the guest bedroom, Evan clung to him. "With you, Uncle Cole."

"Okay."

He set up Evan snugly. The child fell asleep almost right away.

Cole undressed in the bathroom and put on his sweatpants. He climbed into the guest bed beside Evan and stared at the ceiling.

Two children and a man and a woman in one apartment. Like a family.

Exactly like a family, and yet, Cole lay in one bed and Honey in another.

Close, but no cigar.

ON THURSDAY MORNING, a sharp knock on the outside door woke Cole early.

"Stay put," he told Evan.

When he opened the door at the bottom of the stairs, his parents stood on the street, his mother with a puckered mouth.

"So," she declared as though having her suspicions confirmed. "You're sleeping with her."

Cole just managed to restrain himself from lashing out. "Follow me."

Without awaiting a response, he climbed the stairs.

Once at the top, he waited for his aging parents to arrive more slowly. He led them to the guest bedroom. Evan knelt on the bed and scratched his head.

Cole pointed. "That's where I slept last night with Evan."

At that moment, Honey opened the door of her bedroom, the one he'd closed after leaving with Evan last night, thank God. Her hair was a rumpled mess and a crease marred one soft cheek.

Her nightshirt, made of thick cotton and falling to her knees, gave nothing away.

Even his mother had to consider it discreet enough for the children.

She carried Madeline, who rubbed sleep out of her eyes and stared at her grandparents, wary. Her lower lip trembled.

Cole's parents might not be evil, only misguided, but he would never forgive them for making their grievances known in front of the children.

It was obvious to anyone that he and Honey hadn't slept together.

"Honey and Madeline slept in Honey's bed. Madeline needed Honey last night."

"She could have had me," his mother said.

"Since Sandy's death, has Madeline let you hold her?" In the living room, Cole took apart the bed Honey had prepared last night on the sofa and folded the blankets. He gestured for his parents to sit.

His mother shook her head, whether in response to his offer of a seat or to his question about Madeline, Cole wasn't sure, but they both knew the answer.

At the funeral, and afterward, Madeline had turned away from her grandmother. She didn't know her, and Ada was certainly not warm and fuzzy.

"Honey," he said, "do you want to get dressed while I put on coffee?"

After a minute in the washroom to brush her teeth, she went to her bedroom and closed the door. She returned shortly looking like a feminine rock star, in her silver and turquoise jewelry and a yellow blouse.

A long brown skirt trailed to her ankles, and silver sandals covered her feet. Her toenails, he noted, were pink.

A belt hung low on her hips.

God, she was amazing. She'd had no time for makeup, but didn't need it. He thought she was beautiful when she wore it, but she was gorgeous without…and she'd saved him from spending more time alone with his parents than he wanted to.

Madeline ran to Honey and raised her arms. Honey picked her up.

Madeline whispered in her ear. Honey broke out one

of her sunshine smiles. She really needed to bottle, trade-mark and sell them.

"Why, thank you," she said to Madeline. "You look *so* pretty, too."

To Cole, Honey said, "Why don't you go wash up while I feed the children?"

"You sure?" He hated to leave her alone with his hostile parents, hated the disdain on Ada's face when she looked at Honey.

"I've dealt with worse, haven't I?" Honey said, directing a hostile glance of her own toward his mother. "Being a bar owner and all."

Cole couldn't help but smile. He could trust her to stand up to his parents.

In the spare bedroom, he rummaged in his backpack for a clean T-shirt and underwear then snagged his jeans from the back of a wooden chair.

As he entered the bathroom, he heard Honey say, "You are welcome to sit. Coffee's almost ready."

He heard cupboard doors opening and closing and cutlery hitting the counter.

During it all, she kept up a running commentary for the children. "Evan, do you want cereal for breakfast?"

"Yeah! The one with the brown sugar on it."

Hot oatmeal.

"Maddy, what will you have, darling?"

"Her name is Madeline." The palpable outrage in his mother's voice carried to where Cole stood in the bathroom doorway.

What would Honey do?

Next he heard her quiet "Madeline?" followed by, "Maddy?" and then a bubbly "Maddy it is!"

Madeline must have shaken her head no to one and yes to the other.

Cole grinned.

He closed the door and showered.

Ten minutes later, he returned to the living room to find his parents seated, Ada on the sofa and Frank in the only armchair not being used for the fort, with a cup of coffee in his hands and his eyes on Honey.

Unless Cole missed his guess, Frank might already be halfway toward falling in love with her. Cole understood the impulse.

The children ate oatmeal while Honey sipped coffee.

"I wasn't sure what you would want for breakfast," Honey said.

"Let's straighten matters out first." Cole couldn't begin to consider eating while his mother watched like a sour-puss.

"What can I do to convince you that the children are safe here?" Cole directed the question toward his mother. Dad would most likely not be here except for Ada insisting on it. He'd watched his dad be controlled throughout his entire childhood. Was it any wonder Cole resisted marriage in his own life? He'd been controlled too much in childhood and then as a young adult had been the victim of a free spirit who lacked principles.

A human ping-pong ball, he still hadn't sorted out who he was.

Unfortunately, when he'd fallen in love for the first time, it was with a woman as far from his mother in temperament as possible. Now he loved Honey, but didn't know how to reconcile his love for her with his past and his fears. Or how to reconcile the two different parts of her personality.

"There's nothing you can do to convince me the children are safe here," his mother responded to his question. "They don't belong in an apartment above a tavern."

Cole let out a sound of exasperation. "They won't be staying here! I'll be getting a house."

"Why haven't you already? Don't answer. You enjoy spending time here with this tart."

Cole flew, *flew* across the living room to yank his mother to her feet and guide her out of the apartment, but Honey jumped in front of him before he reached Ada. She held him back.

Frank and Ada and the children stared at him with wide eyes.

"She isn't worth it," Honey ground out. "She absolutely is not worth getting into trouble for."

Cole breathed hard. He struggled to pull himself under control. Criminals didn't enrage him as much as his own mother just had. God, it was right that he and Sandy had gotten away from this woman.

Only when he could speak without cursing did he say, "I've been back for only four days. My real estate agent has set up appointments for me. I'm not a miracle worker."

"If you'd stayed at home and married Amber, you and the children would all be where you belong. The children would have a *good* role model in Amber."

Cole's face heated. How dare she insult Honey in her own living room?

His mother opened her mouth to say more, but Cole forestalled her with one step forward. She compressed her lips and crossed her arms over her perfect little white suit jacket.

He couldn't allow her to get away with insulting Honey, who'd done so much for the children. And for him.

Tart.

Cole chewed and swallowed his outrage, but not his sense that he had to do something for Honey, to make up for all of this grief he was causing her.

Cole racked his brain for a solution.

The town loved this woman, and yet his mother thought it was okay to sit in Honey's apartment and call her names.

It didn't take long for Cole to come up with an idea. The townspeople loved Honey. His parents would just have to be shown that.

"Honey, excuse me for a couple of minutes? Please? I have to take care of town business. I won't be long."

"You're leaving? But we haven't resolved anything."

Cole answered his mother. "I have to. I'll only be a couple of minutes."

He shouldn't leave Honey alone with Ada, but he telegraphed a look to her that he hoped she would interpret as *trust me*.

Cole watched her surf through a whole slew of emotions before his pleading look worked and she said, "Okay."

"Could you get the children washed up and get their teeth brushed?"

"Sure." For a split second, a flash of insecurity clouded her features. He didn't blame her. Ada was hostile and the children damaged. Used to having her space to herself, Honey must find this a terrible imposition.

But now Madeline's affection was engaged, and Cole would have to follow through. So was Evan's. Unless Cole missed his guess, the boy adored Honey.

Why couldn't his parents see that? Why couldn't they see what a great person she was?

He turned to his parents. "Don't say a single thing to upset Honey while I'm gone. Not one word."

Across the street in his own apartment, he got on the phone to Travis and described the situation, explaining what he needed.

"I'll get Rachel and the revival committee right on it. How soon?"

"Half an hour? Less? Do you think it can be done?"

"Are you kidding? I swear those women can move mountains."

Cole changed into his sheriff's uniform. Let his parents get a taste of who he really was here.

They still thought of him as the malleable young boy they used to know, but that boy had run away and grown up. He'd rejected their plans and had made a successful life here.

They didn't know him as a man.

His parents should witness his pride in his career…and his respected position among this town's citizens.

Satisfied, Cole returned to Honey's apartment.

His mother flicked her eyes over him then looked away. Unimpressed. Surprise, surprise.

Honey sat at the table waiting for him. The dishes had been washed.

The children were out of sight.

Cole peeked into the cave. There they were. Evan's eyes widened when he saw Cole's uniform, which was more of a reaction than it had elicited from his parents.

What had he expected?

A thick layer of tension suffocated all of the good feelings Honey had built up in the apartment with the children.

Cole couldn't breathe. The old claustrophobia threatened. Damned if he would let it! Damned if he would let *them* control his life again.

"Honey, can you get Madeline dressed?" Cole asked. "I'll take care of Evan."

She reacted to the authority in his voice with a frown but took Madeline to her room without complaint. He understood why. She might not like to take orders, but she would keep the peace in front of his parents for the children's sake.

"Did you think that uniform would impress us?" his mother asked. "You could have been a lawyer. You could have been making decent money, enough to support these children far better than you can now."

"I can support them just fine. Tell me, did Amber marry a lawyer?"

"Of course."

"Who?"

"Gerald Tranchette."

"How long after I left?"

When his mother hesitated to respond, Cole knew it hadn't been long.

"She didn't even wait a year, did she?"

"Eight months," his father said.

"I'm not surprised. She kept pushing me to set a date. She couldn't have cared much for me."

"What do you expect?" his mother asked. "You humiliated her."

"Nothing, and no one, was capable of humiliating Amber LeBlanc. She just substituted one lawyer for another. I assume she got the big house and luxury vehicle she wanted?"

His father nodded.

Honey emerged with Madeline in a pretty white dress and pink sweater.

"We're ready," she said.

She directed her attention to Cole. "Where to?"

"Downstairs."

Surprised, she asked, "To the bar?"

"Yes." Again, he tried to tell her with his eyes that he needed trust.

She got it. "Okay," she said, leading them to the stairs that descended to the street. They could have gone straight from the apartment to the bar by the back staircase, without having to go outside and unlock the front door of the bar, but Cole understood the action. She didn't want to take his parents any farther into her apartment, and her life, than was necessary.

Downstairs, Honey opened up and turned on the lights.

She settled the children into a booth and gave them a bag of chips.

"Potato chips? Really?" His mother frowned.

"They just had a healthy breakfast of oatmeal and orange juice upstairs. Whatever is about to happen down here will probably bore them. They are allowed this small treat."

"Who are you to decide what they are allowed?"

"Let's ask their *guardian*." Honey's gaze shifted from Ada to Cole. "What do you think, Cole? Are they allowed?"

"Yes."

"Why are we here?" his father asked.

The question was repeated on the faces of his mother and Honey.

"You'll find out in a minute."

A knock on the door followed quickly.

When Cole opened it, Travis Read and his family entered. Tori ran to the booth at the back and climbed in beside Madeline.

"Chips!" Tori squealed. "Can I have some?"

Madeline slid the bag to her.

Honey opened another bag and put it on the table, raising her eyebrows at Rachel. *Why are you here?* Rachel shrugged and pulled a bottle of lemonade out of a bag. Honey got some plastic cups from the kitchen and filled them only half-full.

A minute later, Michael Moreno and Samantha Read entered the bar. Sammy kissed her brother Travis's cheek.

"Where are the children?" Honey asked.

"With my neighbor," Michael said. "Figured this was important. Didn't want any distractions."

Violet, Sam Carmichael and his daughter, Chelsea, arrived. Sam leaned against the bar, pulled Vy back against him and rested his hand on her slightly bulging stomach.

Nadine showed up and then Maxine.

Zach Brandt came in quietly, the same way he did everything. Shop owners from all up and down the street arrived. Cole could only guess that they'd closed up for the twenty minutes or so this would take, not that they would miss a lot of sales at nine thirty in the morning.

Udall and Uma Weber from the Double U showed up.

More ranchers came in over the next ten minutes, overwhelming Cole with their generosity of spirit. June was a busy time for a rancher, and leaving to come into town midweek unheard-of.

They talked quietly among themselves. Lester Voile came in chewing on a toothpick, fresh from breakfast at the diner, no doubt.

Cole's parents, a separate dark entity, a vacuum sucking the life out of the room, looked bewildered. Maybe his father more than his mother. Maybe she already had an idea where this was going. She had a sharp mind.

Cole pulled out a couple of chairs from a table in the middle of the room. Frank and Ada sat down.

Jamie and Clint came in with fresh grease under their nails and leaned against the far wall. They must have closed the car repair shop.

One of Cole's deputies, Dane Prescott, in uniform, entered and leaned inside the door against the wall.

Before long, the hooks lining the walls on each side of the door groaned under a surfeit of cowboy hats.

Ranchers who wore those hats more hours of the day than not stood with flattened hair and white foreheads, tanned from the nose down.

At one point, Nadine nodded to Travis. "That's everyone I called."

Maxine and Vy nodded, too, as did Travis and Rachel.

"Now that we're all here," Cole started, but the door burst open and Chet entered. He was probably as tired as Cole, since he'd shut everything down and had locked up after Cole went upstairs last night, yet here he was…

Cole acknowledged him with a nod and started again.

"Thank you all for coming." He felt Honey's eyes on him, curious, and he appreciated her trust in allowing him to use her bar.

"I'd like to introduce my parents to you—Ada and Frank Payette."

Even though they sat stone-faced in the middle of the crowd, there were murmurs of welcome from the crowd.

"I know the rumor mill in Rodeo is as healthy as in any other small town, but I don't know how accurate it is. I want to make sure everyone understands the truth of what's going on." He pointed to himself. "Straight from the horse's mouth."

He glanced at the children. Chet hovered over them. He'd just tied towels around their necks as bibs again and refilled their lemonade glasses.

They played Go Fish with a deck Cole assumed Tori had brought with her, but now they watched the proceedings, their small faces solemn.

Cole caught Chet's eye and nodded toward the kitchen.

Chet said, "You kids know how to make cookies? I need someone to teach me."

Tori dropped her cards onto the table and jumped out of the booth. "I can cook real good, Chet. I hep you."

Cole suspected her quick response had less to do with excitement and more with her desire to escape the tension in the room.

Chet picked up Madeline and held his hand out to Evan. Cole smiled. Madeline was allowing one more person in town to hold her. Slowly, slowly she would get better.

Once Cole heard them murmuring in the kitchen, he continued. "I inherited Evan and Maddy from my sister. She and her husband—"

Without warning, a furious swell of grief grabbed hold of him, shutting down his vocal cords and choking him.

He pressed his lips together, holding in the anger that threatened to spew from him. Life was so goddamned unfair. He counted his breaths to calm himself. Ten. Fifteen. Twenty.

No one said a word. They waited patiently. A man couldn't ask for better friends.

"They were killed in a car accident. I'm the children's guardian now. In their will, Sandy and Dennis left their care to me." His voice broke. He hated to show this weakness. He guessed his friends would find it reasonable given the circumstances, but his mother would use it against him.

"My parents and I are in a legal battle for custody."

Unhappy grumblings flew through the crowd. Cole held up a hand.

"I haven't asked you here to criticize them."

"Why *are* we here?" Michael Moreno asked, his deep voice and solid air calming.

"The children, especially Madeline, have taken a liking to Honey."

"As they should," hardware store owner Cal Frazer said. "All the kids in town love her."

"Yes. What's amazing about this situation in particular is that Madeline hasn't let any woman touch her since her mother died. Not even my mother."

He heard Ada gasp but went on. He had an important point to make and Maddy's feelings were more important than Ada's.

"Maddy will let Honey not only touch her, but hold her and kiss and tuck her into bed at night. Last night Honey let the child share her bed because Madeline was inconsolable in her loss."

Plenty of people nodded, as though it was the least they would expect from Honey.

"Since coming to town, my parents have called Honey's character into question because she owns a bar and has allowed me to sleep on her sofa for the children's sake. A short while ago, in Honey's own apartment, in her home—" Cole's voice shook, but he yanked his rage under control and went on "—my mother called Honey Armstrong a tart."

Gasps echoed through the room. Outrage swelled to fly to the wooden rafters of the ceiling.

"I need all of you to share what you know about Honey, and about how decent she is." He stared at his mother. "Not that it will make a damn bit of difference to my parents, but I need to defend Honey. It makes a difference to *me*."

He met her eyes. She watched him with a bright, damp gaze.

Rachel spoke first, vibrating with indignation. "I've known Honey my entire life. I have two lovely children who love Honey as much as I do. I couldn't ask for a better friend. Calling her a tart was wicked."

Perhaps sensing her mother's tension, Beth, in Rachel's arms, fussed. Travis took her and held her against his chest. She settled.

"I own the diner in town," Vy said. "Honey's one of the best people I know and a damned smart businesswoman."

"I'm a reporter for the town's newspaper. I worked in television in New York City," Nadine said. "You might think we're all country bumpkins here, but we're smart. We know good people. Honey is good."

"Yeah, count me in. I love Honey, too." That last was Max with a belligerent tone. "We also know bad people." She looked down her nose at Ada, because Ada was looking over Max's masculine attire with disdain. Cole almost laughed outright. Max gave as good as she got.

Each woman moved to stand beside Honey.

Vy spoke up again, outlining how Honey gave so much of herself during every weather crisis. "This might look like an ordinary bar, but it's also a town meeting place when people are in need. Honey never says no. Just look at how much she has done for Cole and those children since he arrived home."

She glanced between Cole and Honey. "It isn't because there is a romantic relationship. It's because they are friends. Honey would do anything for a friend."

Cal Frazer interjected, "Remember two summers ago when we had the tornado warning? Myself and all of my customers ran over and hid out in Honey's cellar. So did the other shop owners and clients, because Honey's was large enough to fit us all in."

Jamie and Clint Enright stepped forward to stand in front of Ada. Jamie said, "I don't know why you'd call Honey a tart. I've been trying to get her to go out with me for seven years, ever since Daniel died. She doesn't date anyone. I know. I've been watching."

Cole appreciated Jamie's input, but that seemed creepy. Something must have shown on Cole's face, because Jamie rushed on, "I don't mean in a stalking sense, Sheriff. I just really want to know what her type is if it's not me."

Honey shook her head slightly at Cole, conveying that she didn't find Jamie's behavior creepy. Cole figured it really was purely curiosity on Jamie's part.

"Even if she did or does date a lot, why wouldn't that be her business and not yours?" Clint asked, standing as close to Ada as Jamie did. "Or anybody's. This isn't the '50s, y'know. Women don't have to be ashamed of being sexual creatures."

Vy hooted. A smattering of applause followed. Cole had a new and suddenly deeper respect for Clint.

"Jamie, Clint, step back a bit, okay?" Cole asked. They retreated to a pair of bar stools. "The point here today is not to gang up on my parents. It's to educate them. Frank?

Ada? You've underestimated and maligned a truly beautiful person. You had no right to."

His sweeping arm included everyone in the room. "These are good, good people. The best I've ever met. I'm honored to work for them as their sheriff. Despite their busy lives, especially on a sunny day when many of them should be out attending to their ranch chores, they dropped everything to come into town to defend a friend."

Cole's dad had the grace to look sheepish. Ada, on the other hand, looked more entrenched in her position.

He didn't know why she had to fight so hard, why she needed to win every battle.

Cole turned to everyone and said, "From the bottom of my heart, thank you for doing this for Honey. I know you need to get back to your—"

Michael Moreno interrupted him midsentence. "Hold up, Sheriff."

Cole noted the use of *Sheriff* instead of his name, certain that it signified Michael sending a message to his parents about respect. Gratitude flooded Cole.

He nodded for Michael to continue.

"We've covered how wonderful our own Honey Armstrong is…and how wrong her portrayal by these people was." Another note—Michael hadn't called them Cole's parents. "We need to establish how worthy you are."

Michael looked around the room. "Let me start. I've lived here the whole of my forty years. In that time I've seen some great sheriffs running law enforcement in this county. Even so, I've never known one as good as Cole Payette."

A swell of vocal agreement followed that.

Again, Jamie and Clint stepped forward.

"Cole's a decent guy," Jamie said. "He takes care of this town real well."

"He's tough when he needs to be and shows leniency

when it's called for. He's got a streak of common sense a mile wide."

Talk about miles. A chasm opened up inside Cole at least that wide. He wasn't used to taking praise.

Jamie and Clint might be rough around the edges, which Ada would be sure to note, but they had hearts of gold.

Honor, gratefulness, celebration welled up within Cole, and he fought the hint of moisture gathering in his eyes.

No way would he show vulnerability in front of his parents, not even the good kind.

Pride swelled, not in himself, but in this town and its people. When he'd come here fourteen years ago, he'd chosen well.

Or gotten lucky.

He couldn't imagine living anywhere else.

Ada stood, not quite steady on her feet.

For a moment, Cole felt sorry for her. Maybe this was too much, too many people. Maybe his mother felt bullied.

That hadn't been his intention. He'd simply wanted to defend Honey and to give back to her after all she'd done for him in the past four days.

She should have never had to take a speck of grief from Cole's parents, and he wanted it to stop.

Ada opened her mouth to speak. "Don't expect me to apologize to that woman. Keeping those children upstairs in an *apartment* above a *bar* is wrong. I don't care how good you people believe she is, or how good you think your sheriff is, but nothing here compares to what *I* can offer my grandchildren."

Cole's heart sank. He shouldn't have expected an apology. He shouldn't have expected anything.

Once again, Michael Moreno spoke up. "With all due respect, ma'am, I can see that you have money, but there isn't enough money in the world to replace tenderness and affection and love. You might think you're doing the right thing by those children, but you're dead wrong."

Ada stared daggers at Michael. Michael, about as solid a man as Cole had ever come across, stared right back, but not with anger or hatred. It might be pity or maybe even compassion, because that was the way Michael was built.

"When you take Cole to court for custody of those two little ones, I'll be there to support him." Michael crossed his arms over his solid chest. "I'll testify on his behalf if he'll let me."

The room filled with a groundswell of voices raised in agreement. It seemed they would all do the same.

Cole couldn't speak or he really would crack in front of Ada.

Honey spoke up. "If anyone wants to stay around for coffee, I'll put on a few pots. Otherwise, we're going to take the children out to view real estate."

The townspeople hugged Honey and shook Cole's hand, picked up their cowboy hats and filed out.

The room settled into an uncomfortable, tense silence with Honey and Cole near the door and his parents at the table in the middle of the room.

"I don't know what you hoped to accomplish by that vulgar public display, but you failed."

Cole faced his mother. "If you can't figure out what that was all about, there's no hope for you. Leave."

They stood to go. When his father drew abreast of Cole, he opened his mouth to speak, thought better of it and followed his wife out of the door, disappointing Cole.

He didn't doubt his father had been moved by the impromptu town meeting. Too bad he still didn't have the backbone to buck his wife's will.

His mother said, "See you in court."

His father closed the door behind them.

Nothing had changed. They still planned to wage war.

Chapter Ten

Cole went back to his apartment to change out of his uniform for viewing the house.

In jeans and a white T-shirt, he returned to Honey's apartment.

This whole business of living with children was still so new that he didn't know what was needed.

Doubts assailed him.

What if he bought the house only to find it wasn't suitable?

Julia arrived at Honey's apartment to take them to the house, shooting a speculative look between the two of them, despite the folded bedclothes on the sofa.

Cole wanted the children to see the house before he committed to it, so he told Julia they would meet over there.

They drove over in his truck, Honey with them. It took all of three minutes.

A two-story solid-brick home with three bedrooms, the house stood on a large treed lot on a side street off Main. A broad, deep veranda ran along the front of the house, an inviting spot on a hot summer evening, no doubt.

Honey seemed out of sorts, even with the children.

Used to her sunny ways, he wondered if he and the children had worn her out.

HONEY COULDN'T NAME what was wrong with her.

She wasn't usually in a bad mood.

It wasn't the children. She loved having them around. For so many years, since her mother's death, she'd lived in that big old apartment alone, never once unhappy, only occasionally feeling a lack in her life.

She and Daniel had never lived together.

Now she dreaded the emptiness after the children left. This house would be perfect for them. Of course Cole would buy it.

How could he not?

As early as this weekend, these rooms could ring with Evan's shouts and Cole's heavy tread, while Honey's apartment would suddenly be bereft and empty in a way it had never been before.

Their footsteps echoed from the high ceilings of vacant rooms. This house needed a family.

Other than needing a good cleaning, some small repairs and new appliances, it was perfect.

Evan ran from one end of the long hallway to the other shouting, "Look at me!"

He took off his shoes and skated across the floor in his socks, an ice dancer without skates. "Look what I can do."

"Let's go upstairs," Cole said. "Take a look at the bedrooms."

Three good-size bedrooms and a bathroom bracketed the long hallway.

The children could have their own rooms. The one room that ran across the front of the house would hold Cole's king-size bed easily.

She could see them all living here happily.

And that was when it hit her.

Like a ton of bricks, the thought came unbidden. *I don't want them to leave me. I would keep them forever.*

Madeline skipped and hummed from room to room.

Evan skated on the old hardwood floors upstairs. The floors creaked beneath their feet.

Cole asked her opinion of the house and the yard. He discussed his furniture needs.

When Cole and the children moved in here, her apartment would be changed forever. Honey would never be able to see it in the same light again.

These children had happened to her, and their presence could never be undone.

She could already feel loneliness settling in.

For a woman who treasured independence, and who filled spare moments with activity, she understood with bleak conviction that there was not enough activity on the earth to make up for losing these children.

And be honest, Honey. For losing Cole.

Shocked, she stood at a window and stared at the overgrown yard below, desperate to hide her burgeoning feelings from Cole.

Where had they come from?

From spending so much time with him, helping him through an emotional trial. From recognizing everything that was good and wonderful about Cole. His decency. His love for the children. His conviction that he was doing the right thing in taking on his wealthy parents. His courage in having broken free of their control.

As well, there was his body. For the first time in a long time, her body ached to satisfy unused muscles. She wanted sex. She wanted it with Cole.

She would love to start with a hug.

Just one hug.

Turning away from the window, she put on a bright, fixed smile so he wouldn't see what she was feeling.

If he knew, he might withdraw from her. She would miss seeing him and Evan and Madeline.

He was smart, she'd learned, and intuitive.

As well, she'd gone down this road with a lawman before and the grief when he'd been killed had been tremendous. It had taken her a long time to get over it. She couldn't take the chance of going through that again. She wasn't strong enough.

That brought up a thought…what was Cole's plan for the children if anything should happen to him?

She should discuss it with him. Or maybe not. He'd come to her for help. She'd given it. Soon he and the children would live here on their own, without her. What he did next was none of her business.

Strolling through the rooms, she planned her strategy for survival in this brave new world when she felt anything but brave.

Honey, who barely knew what the word *insecurity* meant, didn't know how to go ahead into the future.

She'd never known a moment of self-pity, not even when her mother—and then Daniel—had died and left her alone. But now she wanted to cry.

She wanted the children. She wanted Cole.

And they were leaving her.

"The house is good. Sound." Cole led the way downstairs. "Let's check out the yard."

Outside, the grass grew far too high. Remnants of a kitchen garden had long ago lost the fight to a hostile weed takeover.

Evan ran ahead, whacking at the grass with a stick that at one time must have been a plant stake.

"It isn't too far from the sheriff's office," Cole said.

"Not too far," Honey managed to respond.

Cole held Madeline's hand but picked her up where the grass grew too tall for her. "If I get an emergency call, it won't take long for someone to come out to watch the children while I head off to work."

Honey murmured her agreement, unable to speak in case he heard her desperate unhappiness.

Cole, Evan and Madeline had to start their new lives together soon. It made perfect sense.

Still, Honey brooded. She had never been a brooder. She had become, just this moment while walking this land behind the sturdy house with a newfound family, a world-class brooder.

"Can I buy this week and be in by the weekend?" Cole asked Julia. "By Sunday?"

"I'm sure that can be arranged. The Ashers are motivated sellers."

She quoted him a figure and Cole nodded.

It would suit them. Honey had no doubt of that.

She wondered if he could afford the house.

He must have read her mind. "I haven't had much to spend my money on over the years. I've got a decent down payment. Plus, Sandy and Dennis had good life insurance policies. We won't be wealthy like my parents, but we'll be fine."

Turning to walk back to the house, she studied the white clapboard siding and pictured herself in the window on the second floor looking out over new-mown grass and a kitchen vegetable garden and a flower bed planted purely for frivolous pleasure, and maybe wildflowers scattered for Madeline, with a weeping willow in the distance and yellow wheat fields beyond that.

Her bed, with all its lace, would look amazing in one of those upstairs bedrooms with the dark, creaky old hard-wood floor.

But she wouldn't be here…and neither would her bed.

"This place will work out for us," Cole rumbled beside her.

Yes, it would all work out for Cole and the children, Honey thought glumly.

But not for me.

THE HOUSE NEEDED to be cleaned, so Cole decided they would impose on Honey for a couple of nights more and move into the house on Sunday.

He called Julia to confirm that she had managed to hire people to scour the house on Friday and Saturday.

A bunch of teenagers were hired to clear the grounds and get rid of anything Cole might not want his children exposed to. He wouldn't be surprised to learn kids had been hanging out in the backyard. There could be liquor bottles or broken glass hidden in the long grass.

He'd never caught anyone there, but it was best to make sure.

In the diner, Lester Voile said he would bring his riding mower out and mow the property free of charge.

"God, no," Cole said. "I'll pay you for your time and your gas."

"You done enough for this town, Sheriff," Lester countered.

"I was only doing my job."

"Nope. You go above and beyond. All the time. Through every snowstorm. You're one of the good ones, Sheriff Payette. I won't take a cent from you."

Cole accepted graciously. "I'll hire a couple of young guys to rake up the grass after it's mowed."

"Yep. Good idea. It's long." Lester chewed on a generous mouthful of jalapeño mac and cheese. After swallowing, he said, "I have an attic full of old furniture. You need anything?"

"I'd like to look, if you don't mind."

"Don't mind at all. Would be nice to see some of it being used."

Michael Moreno, Travis Read, Zach Brandt and Jamie and Clint Enright all agreed to help him move his furniture in on Sunday. Every one of them owned a pickup truck, as did Cole, so he wouldn't have to rent a moving van.

Chet offered to cook for them, if Honey didn't mind him using the bar's kitchen.

Of course she didn't mind, and she told him to use the bar's food supplies, too. She ordered Cole to not buy food.

Will offered to make enough pies for everyone as long as Violet didn't mind if he used the kitchen in the diner.

She didn't, of course.

Cole walked away from the diner thinking he was the most blessed man on earth.

If only he could figure out what was wrong with Honey.

Only two more nights of being too close to the terrible temptation of Honey and her beautiful body and spirit. Two more nights to lie on the sofa and know that she was only a hallway away, but as unavailable as a woman could be.

While Honey watched the children, Cole visited a lawyer's office to start the purchase, contingent on a home inspection, and the bank to apply for a mortgage. He arranged for insurance on the house.

A home inspector would do a walk-through first thing tomorrow morning. If he approved, the sale would proceed.

Feeling a little buzzed, like he'd drunk too much coffee, he returned to Honey's apartment.

Whoo. In a few days, he would be a homeowner.

Honey went down to the bar at three.

Cole took the children to the Summertime Diner for dinner before returning to the apartment.

When the music was turned on downstairs, the children didn't seem to mind. They were in bed asleep by eight.

Cole picked up a book, but he couldn't concentrate.

Strange to not be downstairs occupying his bar stool on a Friday evening. He wouldn't be able to help at the bar tomorrow night, either.

His life had been altered permanently, and he couldn't imagine how his weekends would look from now on. Not that they'd ever been exciting, but he'd liked his Friday and Saturday nights helping Honey.

In the future, he would see less of her. Already, on this first weekend, he felt the loss.

At the sound of angry raised voices, Cole rushed downstairs to find three men seated on stools on the stage.

A woman sat on a stool off to the side.

Damn. He'd forgotten about matchmaking night. The last Friday of every month, Honey held this special night, her chance to try to match up a man and woman in town.

Two of the male participants were getting rowdy, yelling at each other. He understood why. The woman seated off to the side with a list of questions for the bachelors was Eva Cantrell, and the two men fighting over her both had a crush on her.

What had Honey been thinking, putting those two onstage together?

Cole stalked the length of the room to stand in front of them. When they noticed him, they stopped fighting.

"We got a problem here?" he asked.

"No, sir, Sheriff."

"Do I need to call out the deputies?"

"Nope."

"Good."

He felt a tug on his arm. Honey, dragging him away. In the hallway behind the bar, he confronted her.

"Damn it, Honey, this happens every single month. Why do you keep holding these stupid matchmaking nights?"

"They aren't stupid, Cole. They're fun. It's only once a month, for Pete's sake."

"There's always a fight."

"It wasn't a fight. It was an argument. Did you see anyone throw a punch?"

No, he hadn't.

She pointed to the crowd. "Does anyone look seriously angry? No. They're having fun."

After her gloom of the past couple of days, Honey looked sunny and all smiles. "I like bringing couples together and so do my customers. They find my questions for the bachelors fun and entertaining. I love these nights."

"You're too sentimental."

"No such thing, Cole."

"You're too romantic."

"Again, no such thing."

"Honey, this has got to stop. It makes my job hard."

"You're off duty. Get your deputies to handle it, but only when there's a real fight. Otherwise, Chet and I can take care of things. These are my people, Cole. Your deputies are only one phone call away, if needed."

She had him there, but he rallied.

"How can I have a moment's peace when there's the possibility of a fight?"

Honey shrugged before returning to pulling pitchers of draft beer. "I don't know, Cole. Maybe go back upstairs and try to ignore this?"

This was a side of Honey he wasn't crazy about. Was she being irresponsible? Or was he overreacting?

He stomped upstairs, his thoughts keeping time with his steps.

A loud burst of laughter from the crowd swept up the stairs.

Okay, maybe Honey wasn't being unreasonable. Maybe it was a good business decision. The crowd sure did appreciate matchmaking night.

He couldn't think straight where Honey was concerned.

She turned him inside out, making him dream of things that didn't have much chance of success.

ON SATURDAY AFTER breakfast at the diner, while Honey slept in, he and the children walked to the house and found a beehive of activity.

Apparently, the kids he'd hired had done a good job of cleaning up, because Lester had just finished mowing the entire lot without problems.

Four teenagers moved in to rake up while Lester rode his mower onto his trailer.

Cole shook his hand. "Thanks, Lester. You did a great job."

"My pleasure, Sheriff. You need anything else, let me know."

Inside the house, the army of cleaners had done a great job, as well. The floors shone and the appliances were spotless.

The following morning after breakfast and church services, Cole's friends would get together and deliver his furniture, plus what he'd selected from Lester's attic. Since Lester's children were fully grown and living in different states, he had single beds to spare for Evan and Madeline.

Cole took the kids to the grocery store, where they picked up lunch to share with Honey.

"It's our last day with her, so let's give her a special lunch, okay?"

When Maddy started to object to them moving out of Honey's, he pointed to the baked goods in one of the cases to distract her and said, "What would Honey like for dessert today?"

"Cake," Maddy said.

"What do you think, Evan?"

"Cake."

"Okay, we just have to decide which one." He vetoed a

sheet cake that could feed a dozen and suggested instead a chocolate layer cake on which they all agreed. Evan liked the puffs of chocolate icing around the edges and Maddy liked the pink and blue sprinkles.

Back at Honey's, they found her vacuuming.

"I should do that," Cole said.

"Why?"

"Because we've been here all week. A lot of that dust was tracked in by us."

"Cole, I vacuum every Saturday morning. If you want to help, you can strip the beds and throw the sheets in the washing machine with the towels we've all used this week."

She directed him to a small room at the back of the apartment, where a stacked washer and dryer set stood neatly against one wall.

Making a game of it, he had the children gather their washcloths and towels while he tore apart their beds.

In the doorway of Honey's bedroom, he halted. "Um... Honey?"

She'd finished vacuuming and was putting away groceries. "Yeah?"

"Can you come here for a sec?"

She approached down the hallway. "What is it?"

"Can you get your sheets for me?"

She looked at him and then at her bed. A small smile curved up the corners of her pretty lips. Yeah, he was too shy to touch her bed linens, only because he'd seen her lying in them with his children. He'd seen how beautiful she looked amid all of that icing-sugar lace.

A few minutes later, she joined him in the small laundry room and started up the washer.

"Let's have lunch. Then we'll put the children's dirty clothes in. They'll go to the new house with clean outfits."

Good idea. Maddy and Evan were on their last pairs of clean underwear.

Honey made a big deal out of dessert. "This is beautiful. Which one of you children chose this lovely cake?"

Both of them raised their hands.

"Well, you did an amazing job."

While she dished it out, Cole changed the load to the dryer and put in the children's clothes to wash.

When he returned to the kitchen, the table had plates of cake in four spots. The children had glasses of milk, while Honey had put out blue mugs of coffee for the adults.

"Cheers," she said.

They raised their half-full plastic cups and clicked them against the adults' coffee mugs and giggled.

Cole couldn't help but feel a sense of loss—tomorrow he would be alone in that house without Honey's help with the children.

He would miss this feeling of belonging, this perfect camaraderie.

Following fast on the heels of that was panic.

God. He would have to do it all alone.

Honey watched him, maybe guessing what was going through his mind.

She covered his hand with hers. "It will work out, Cole."

He wished from the bottom of his heart that he could give in to his desire for her and tell her how he felt. Could they make it work?

Old betrayals—his parents in town raising memories he wished would stay buried—held him back.

He dropped her hand and ate his cake, but it tasted like sawdust. It must have been only his taste buds not working. Everyone else loved it.

THAT EVENING AFTER putting the children to bed, Cole played games on Honey's computer.

When he tired of that, he changed into his sweats and watched TV.

The night was hot, summer having hit with a vengeance. Despite air-conditioning, humidity seemed to seep in through the walls.

He pulled off his T-shirt, turned off the TV and leaned back onto his pillow. He didn't notice what time he fell asleep on the sofa.

His cell phone buzzed.

He glanced out the window, dark save for the streetlamp. Silence downstairs alerted him to the lateness of the hour.

The bar was closed for the night. The noise up here wasn't as bad as he would have thought it would be. He'd slept through the Saturday night crowd.

Something had awakened him, though.

As sheriff, he'd grown used to being called at all hours. But it hadn't been a call. He scrubbed the sleep out of his eyes and checked the time. Two a.m.

He recognized Honey's number. What did she need? He opened the text.

The lone word on his screen angered him.

Hel

C'mon, Honey. Hello at two in the morning?

With no small amount of impatience, he scrubbed his eyes again, more forcefully this time. He texted, What do you need? and waited.

No response.

It's late. Why did you text?

Still no response.

That's when it hit. It wasn't Hello! It was Help.

Chapter Eleven

He took the back stairs two at a time, bare feet slipping, and hit the bottom at a run. He pulled up, the place dark save for a couple of dim lights at the front end of the hallway in the bar proper.

He noted silence in the kitchen. Darkness. Chet was gone.

Cole reached for his gun, an automatic gesture. He didn't have it. He'd refused to bring it into Honey's apartment. Why would he need it? He wasn't back at work until Monday.

He tiptoed down the hallway and peeked around the corner into the bar.

There, behind the bar, a man he'd never seen before had Honey up against the wall trying to kiss her. Rage filled him.

Honey's hand in his hair pulled the stranger's head away from her. Her other hand between them tried to push him away.

The guy was huge. He leaned away from her and tried to catch her wrists. She fought hard.

"Give in." The guy had the nerve to laugh. "You know you want it. You been teasing me all night."

"I said no."

Cole's vision misted, narrowed to a single hot target.

"Tease" was the last word the man spoke before Cole grabbed him by the back of his jacket and the seat of his pants and tossed him over the bar.

The guy landed on the floor with a loud *thud*. The floor shook.

"Are you all right?" Cole asked Honey, but she wasn't. He could see in her wide eyes terror had a hold of her.

Cole rounded the bar just as the stranger stood and came at him swinging.

Cole veered away and the punch glanced off his cheek. He coldcocked the guy who went down with the solid thump of dead weight.

Fear and adrenaline arcing through him, lost to reason or sense, Cole picked him up by the shirtfront to deliver another blow when his arm was grasped and held from behind.

"Goddamn it," he roared and turned to give whoever it was a piece of his mind. Honey, hair wild, had both arms wrapped around his forearm.

"Don't, Cole." For someone who had recently been attacked, and whose eyes were still scared, her voice came out surprisingly steady. "He's unconscious. If you hit him again, it will be assault."

It took a minute for the red clouds of anger to clear.

"He's out," Honey said, hair quivering with the tremors that ran through her. "He's harmless now, Cole."

Panic released its hold. He'd saved Honey.

"I was terrified. When I saw him mauling you—"

She touched his cheek where the guy's fist had grazed it before Cole had knocked him out. He winced.

"You're going to be bruised."

He shook his head, impatient. "Doesn't matter."

"It does." She kissed it gently. "I was terrified, Cole."

"Honey." His voice broke. "Jesus, Honey."

She was in his arms and he was kissing her, holding

her tightly enough for them to become one, passion fueled by the horror of what might have been if he hadn't been upstairs.

He pulled back to stroke her cheek, her hair, to breathe in the fragrance of her neck, then arched her against him again with an arm around her waist.

"I won't lose you, Honey. I won't see you harmed." He'd lost too much. He refused to lose another loved one. He squeezed her until she whimpered, letting go so quickly she almost fell.

Grasping her arms, he whispered, "I'm sorry. I wouldn't hurt you for the world."

"Cole, I know that." Stepping away from him, she pushed her hair away from her face. Her hands shook. "We have to deal with him."

"Where's your phone?"

She retrieved it from the floor behind the bar. God, she'd probably had only a second to send him that text.

"How did you manage to text me?"

"I'll explain it all when the deputy gets here. You'd better call him before that idiot comes around."

Before Cole had the chance, he took a direct hit to his left temple.

Honey screamed.

The guy had lunged up from the floor. Cole turned before the guy could hit him again, but he reeled, dizzy. He managed to dodge a huge fist but went down on one knee. Before the guy could haul off and punch him again, Cole pulled his feet out from under him then stood in front of him, fists raised and ready.

A big guy, he hit hard. The floor vibrated under the bare soles of Cole's feet.

The man lashed out with a boot and Cole jumped away but came back swinging, managing to land a punch that had nose bones crunching under his fist.

The stranger leaped to his feet and grabbed him around the ribs, squeezing hard. Cole hit the guy in the side of the head. Cole's breath went shallow. Stars danced in his vision.

Still he hit and hit, then heard a loud smash and was sprayed by liquid.

Honey stood with a broken vodka bottle in her hand. The man had blood and vodka pouring from a scalp wound.

Someone hammered on the front door.

"Who's that?" Cole spun around.

"Chris Mortimer," Honey said. The deputy on duty tonight. "I called as soon as he hit you the second time." She opened the door, and Chris burst inside.

"What happened?"

Honey started to tell him. Her knees buckled. Cole caught her.

"I can't breathe," she whispered.

She didn't lose consciousness, but Cole had seen this reaction to shock plenty of times.

When she could stand on her own two feet again, he put his hands on her waist and lifted her onto the bar.

She protested. "What are you doing?"

"Checking you out." Fingers gentle, he pushed her hair back and studied her face for bruising. A red mark marred one cheek. "Did he *hit* you?"

"He slapped me."

Fury arose in Cole again, but he controlled it.

He probed her scalp. "He was pushing you hard against the wall. Did he hurt your head?"

"A bit. My back hurts, but I don't think I'm bruised."

Cole's thumb brushed her bottom lip and held it down. There, on the tender flesh inside, was blood. He realized he'd tasted it when he kissed her. She'd been cut by her own teeth.

"Bastard." That one word was only the start. His pungent swearing lasted until Chris cleared his throat. He stood over the prone stranger.

Chris had already rolled the man over and cuffed him.

"Better get the paramedics out to check on him," Cole said. "If he gets the all clear, book him and put him in a cell. If not, follow him to the hospital."

Chris called for help and then said, "Fill me in on what happened."

"I was asleep upstairs on the sofa." Cole needed that to be clear so he wouldn't smear Honey's reputation. A thought occurred to him. "The kids are upstairs alone. If they wake up with neither of us there, they'll be frightened."

"I'll call Nadine," Honey said. "She's only five minutes away. She'll sit with them."

Honey moved to get down off the bar. Cole lifted her down. She clutched the phone in a grip that turned her knuckles white.

Minutes later, Nadine slipped in through the front door. Cole explained why they needed her. After a hug and kiss for Honey, Nadine scooted upstairs.

Chris took off his jacket and hung it over the back of a chair. Notepad in one hand and a pen in the other, he approached Honey but kept a respectful distance when he noticed her shaking.

"Who is he?" the deputy asked Honey.

"I don't know. I never saw him before he came into the bar tonight. He said he was passing through."

"You want to tell me what happened before Cole got on the scene?"

Cole raised his hand. "She shouldn't be questioned until we get her attacker out of here."

"Now!" Honey said. "I'm telling it now." Her teeth chattered.

Cole glanced at Chris who shrugged a little helplessly.

"Okay. Do it now," Cole said. "In that case, I need to leave so you can question her privately. After that, I'll give my statement separately away from Honey."

Chris nodded. "Way it should be."

But when Cole turned to leave, Honey grasped his arm, frantic. "Don't leave. Stay with me."

"Not the way it's done," Chris said, looking as lost as Cole felt. "But…"

Cole nodded. "Let's do what's best for Honey."

They looked at her and she picked up her story.

"I told everyone I was closing. They filed through the front door. I locked it. I hadn't seen this guy for a good forty minutes. I thought he'd already left. Then Chet called from the back that he was heading home. I locked the back door behind him and then returned to the front."

Honey sounded unemotional, but a fine tremor disrupted her voice.

Cole took her hand in his, squeezed and held on.

"A second later he came out of the back hallway," she continued. "My guess is he'd been hiding in the washroom waiting for the place to close. I told him he had to leave. He said—"

She shuddered.

To hell with rules and best practices. Cole lifted her into his arms and sat on a chair with her on his lap. Snagging Chris's jacket, he wrapped it around her, holding her close to still her shivers.

Now that the worst was over, Cole felt cold, too, starting in his head where the worst of his rage transmuted into fear of what might have happened to Honey. He held onto her as tightly as she would allow.

Honey didn't resist. She leaned against him.

Chris crouched in front of her. "What did he say?"

"He said he wasn't leaving until he got what he wanted."

"And what did you understand that to mean?"

"Sex, even if I wasn't willing."

"How do you know even if you weren't willing?"

She sat forward. "I know, okay?"

"Easy, Honey. I believe you, but I need to write down everything he actually said and did."

Cole urged her back against his chest and wrapped his arms around her.

"I said no."

"You definitely said no. Actually said it."

"Yes. Point-blank."

Chris nodded. "Good, Honey. That's real good."

"What happened next?" Cole asked.

"I could see where it was heading, so I ran behind the bar to text Cole. I didn't even get the word finished. I don't know how Cole knew what I meant."

"I figured it out."

"Why didn't you phone him?" Chris asked.

Honey stared, stricken. "I don't know." Her eyes welled with tears.

"Easy," Chris said. "Our actions don't always make sense in the heat of the moment."

She nodded and sniffed.

"What happened next?" Chris pressed.

"He grabbed me, threw me against the wall and started molesting me."

"Okay. Anything else you want to add?"

"He kept trying to make passes at me all night. I resisted every single one. I did *not* tease him."

"Of course not, Honey. You never do."

"Are you mocking me, Chris?"

He drew back, shocked. "God, no. Why would you think that?"

"I'm sorry!" She reached out a hand to him. "Chris, I'm sorry. I'm so rattled. I'm sensitive, I guess. I've always been able to handle the men in the bar. I thought I was strong, but I couldn't fight him off."

"Look at the size of him, Honey. You weren't going to win with him."

Honey started to tremble again, and Cole prodded Chris with his bare toes. "You're scaring her."

"I can't say anything right tonight," Chris grumbled.

"I'm on edge, too," Cole said. "Sorry."

Chris held up both hands. "This was a rough incident."

"Wha' happened?" The man on the floor stirred.

Chris stood up to give the man an eyeful of his uniform.

"What's going on?" the stranger asked. "I can't move my hands."

"You're handcuffed and under arrest for attempted sexual assault."

"Assault! Who'd I assault? Not that bartender. If she said so, she's lying."

"I saw you, bud," Cole said. "I saw her trying to push you away. I heard her say no. You didn't stop. That's sexual assault."

"Stupid bitch."

Cole jumped up from the chair, dropping Honey to her feet.

Chris stood in front of him like an immovable wall and caught Cole's fist in his. "You won't do this, Cole. I won't let you throw away your career on this piece of useless crap."

God, where Honey was concerned Cole had no control over his emotions. He never reacted this way to crime in town. He kept his feelings under control and kept a cool head. Thank God for Chris tonight.

Honey reached for Cole's face and nudged it down, forcing him to meet her eye. "Don't. Please. Don't get into trouble over this."

He relented and eased back.

A hard banging at the door startled them.

"That was fast," Chris said. He opened the door for the paramedics. "Check this guy out," he directed. "Let me know if he's well enough to spend the night in jail or if he needs a hospital visit."

They rolled in a gurney and checked out the prisoner. "You said he lost consciousness? Twice? He probably has a concussion. Who hit him? You, Mortimer?"

"Nah. Sheriff Payette."

The medic shot him an assessing look. "No wonder he's got a concussion."

"For God's sake, get him out of here," Cole said. "I don't care where you take him. Just get him out of Honey's bar."

They heaved him onto the gurney with Chris's help and rolled him out.

"I'll take my jacket now and follow the ambulance."

Honey handed him his coat. "Thanks for coming so quickly, Deputy Mortimer."

"My pleasure, Honey. I'm glad Cole was here to save you from serious harm."

"Me, too," Honey breathed.

The door closed behind him, and they were left in blessed silence.

Cole locked the door, sat Honey back down and went to the bar. He returned with two shot glasses of brandy.

"Drink," he ordered.

He threw his own back. It burned all the way down. Just what he needed.

Honey sipped hers. When she finished, she handed him her glass. He left them both on the bar, returned and picked her up to carry upstairs.

"I can walk!"

"Hush. Let me take care of you. Just for a minute."

She snuggled against him, out of character for her. Cole liked holding her.

In her bedroom, he laid her on the lace comforter, amid her mass of pillows.

No children in her bed tonight. Without Honey at home to crawl into bed with, they'd fallen asleep in the other bedroom.

"Get dressed for bed. I'll tell Nadine she can leave and lock up behind her."

In the living room, Nadine sat on the only armchair not being used for the cave. She jumped to her feet.

"Is Honey okay?"

"She's badly shaken."

"Was she—" Nadine couldn't say that one thing that Cole imagined every woman feared.

"No. I got down there in time."

"How did you know?"

He picked up his cell phone from the coffee table and showed her Honey's message.

"That was enough?" Nadine looked skeptical.

"It took me a minute, but I figured Honey wouldn't text hello at two in the morning."

"No. I guess not." Nadine pushed messy red hair away from her face.

He walked her downstairs. After letting Nadine out and watching her walk down the block and enter her apartment above the newspaper office, Cole locked the door. Back upstairs, he checked on the children and sighed on finding them both sound asleep. Thank God they hadn't seen or heard any of that ugliness.

Hovering in the hallway outside their doorway, he hesitated. He wanted to see Honey. He had to make sure she was okay.

The door to her bedroom stood ajar. She wouldn't have left it open if she were undressed. Right?

Quietly, he approached and nudged it open.

She lay on her back with the covers drawn up under her

armpits, staring at the ceiling. About to turn away, he took a second look. Her fists clenched the comforter.

He stepped closer. Silent tears leaked from the corners of her eyes.

"Aw, Honey. I'm sorry." He sat on the edge of the mattress to pull her into his arms. "Don't cry. God, don't cry."

Her arms wrapped around him. She cried quietly for a while. When she stopped, she whispered, "Why are you apologizing? You did nothing wrong."

"It's this whole situation. If not for the children being here, I would have been downstairs at the bar protecting you until closing time."

"Is that why you come on the weekends? To protect me?"

"Yeah," he breathed. He wrapped one lock of hair around his finger. It turned out to be every bit as soft as he'd imagined. "I know you're strong. I know you value independence. But... I worry..."

She touched his chest with fingers that lightly caressed his skin, and he was lost.

"I can't lose you. I care about you. I can't lose another woman I lo—"

Her tears started in earnest, wet and hot on Cole's shoulder.

"What's wrong? Is it delayed shock? Are you hurt?"

"No," she wailed and tried to hide her face against his chest.

He held her until she cried herself out, angry and frustrated that he couldn't do more.

She wouldn't look at him. She wouldn't let him ease her face away from his chest.

Cursing, he said, "Don't hide, Honey. Please. Talk to me."

"God, Cole." She sniffed and pulled herself together. "I heard what you almost said."

"I didn't—"

"Stop, okay?" She put her fingers against his lips. "It's time we started being honest with each other."

How could he be honest? How could he lay himself bare? What was the point of honesty when nothing could ever come of it?

Sometimes she controlled too much. Sometimes she was too free-spirited. Most of the time she was wonderful. But Cole wasn't. He didn't know how to accept Honey as a harmonious whole.

The arrival of his parents in town had brought up all the old neuroses. He couldn't trust his instincts. What if he became involved with Honey and found out he was every bit as screwed up as he'd been with his parents? Or with Shiloh?

He'd never had a healthy relationship in his life.

The only one that had come close to healthy was with Sandy, but part of that was from having shared an unhealthy childhood.

He didn't know how to do healthy.

He kissed Honey with every bit of emotion he had then left her bed abruptly to finish his night alone on the sofa.

Honey stood in the shower. Water poured over her shoulders and back, as hot as she could take it. If she soaked long enough, maybe she could wash away the feeling of that animal's hands on her last night.

"Honey?" Cole knocked on the door. "That shower's been running a long time. You okay?"

"Yes." Her voice came out ragged. She cleared her throat. "I'm okay."

She sensed him hovering on the other side of the door.

"Cole, I'm fine, really."

Finally, he said, "I'll make you breakfast."

"I'll be out soon."

She pulled herself together, dressed and ate the breakfast Cole made for her.

Disoriented, she didn't feel like herself. For the first time in...ever...she wanted to get out of this building.

They took the children to the house.

"Are you sure you're up to this after last night?"

"Yes, I am. Honest." She might have had one of her worst experiences in her bar, but no way was Honey letting this affect the children.

She pretended everything was okay for them.

While Cole and his friends retrieved his belongings from his dingy apartment, Honey entertained the children.

When they moved his furniture in, it barely filled one room.

Then they left to get Lester's furniture.

There was still so much more Cole needed to get, so much he still had to do to turn this place into a home.

Just as Honey had that thought, an army of women showed up in a half dozen cars.

She didn't know who had organized it, but no one had told her. She guessed it was because they knew she would be watching the children while Cole moved furniture.

They were all over him and he laughed and talked and shared jokes.

They hung curtains and brought pretty cushions for his old leather sofa. They set his table with place mats and napkins.

They brought food and drinks.

Throughout, Cole basked in their affection.

Only Honey felt left out.

She knew what she would face at home that evening—emptiness and loss.

Before Cole had brought her two children to love, she'd been happy.

Her life had been full. Or so she'd thought.

In his bedroom, she stared at his oversize, masculine bed.

She thought of him sitting on her bed last night and holding her while she cried. They should have done more. They should have given in to temptation and given each other if not love then at least comfort.

Before Cole, she'd never realized how perfectly she'd designed her lacy nest for lovemaking.

All of this time, she'd thought her goal had been to create her own little cave, like the one the children had created, for sleep. For rest. For recuperation.

But no. She had designed it, she realized now, to cradle her and her lover in the act of lovemaking. Cole, being Cole, would never make love to Honey.

She didn't know why that hurt when she'd never thought of him romantically before...and when she feared becoming involved with lawmen.

Good for him, that he had that much self-discipline, but he'd left *her* in need—and she didn't know how to fill it.

Her cell rang, and she answered.

"Honey, I just heard. Are you okay?" Violet, with her characteristic blunt nature, peppered Honey with all kinds of questions.

"Vy, slow down. Yes, I'm fine."

"Are you sure? You don't sound quite yourself."

"I'm not, but I will be okay."

"You will be, because all of your friends are going to make sure of it. The guys have agreed to babysit this evening and we're taking you out."

"No. I don't think I can face a restaurant or a party. I can't go out."

"I don't mean that. We're having a picnic. We're going down to the lake just like we did all last summer."

A picnic down by the lake with her friends. The temptation was great.

She knew what it meant…a couple of bottles of wine, great food al fresco and a dip in the water. It had been so hot lately. The water must be warm for swimming by now.

Her friends would soothe her and ease her mind after last night's ordeal. How like them to rally around her. A woman couldn't ask for better friends.

Plus, it would get her out for the evening so she wouldn't have to face her apartment alone. Had it only been one week since the children had arrived? How had she become attached so quickly?

"Yes," she said. "I would like that a lot, Vy. What should I bring?"

"Nothing. We've got it all handled. Just show up at our favorite spot at seven. Okay?"

"You got it."

Honey stayed long enough to see how the house looked after the additional furniture from Lester Voile's place came. She commandeered Zach Brandt to watch the children then left.

Too many people. Too much activity. Too much camaraderie.

Plus, she just couldn't say goodbye to the children.

She'd never been a coward. She was today.

Maybe it was last night's shock that had left her vulnerable, maybe it was having the children and then losing them, or maybe it was the desire for Cole that she found harder and harder to resist.

Back in her apartment, she crawled into bed to sleep away some of the day.

TRAVIS READ CALLED COLE.

"Hey, Tori is saying she'd really like to visit with Evan

and Maddy since her mother's not going to be home to-night."

"Rachel's going out?"

"Yeah, you know, with the other women of the revival committee. For a picnic by the lake."

No, he didn't know. Honey had left earlier without saying goodbye.

"Anyway," Travis was saying, "how about you and the children come for supper? Sam's bringing Chelsea."

Madeline would love that. She'd liked Chelsea. Plus, it would relieve Cole of dealing with his first evening alone in the house with the children.

They drove to Travis's comfy Victorian for a supper that the children, and Cole, enjoyed.

Cole couldn't stop worrying about Honey, though. He remembered the women going to Cloud Lake a few times last summer, and where their favorite spot was. The lake was a bit more isolated than he'd like, being off the highway out of town.

After dessert, Travis settled the children in front of the TV to watch a movie.

They snuggled on the sofa with a couple of bowls of popcorn. Cole was relieved to see Evan and Maddy becoming more comfortable with every passing day in Rodeo.

"Listen," Cole said quietly to Travis and Sam in the kitchen, "they're happy watching the movie. Do you mind if I go out for a while?"

Travis's brows shot up. "You got somewhere important to be?"

"I just need to do something."

"Okay. Sure. Go."

Sam nodded. "We can take care of the kids."

Cole left through the back door so Madeline and Evan wouldn't see him go. He didn't plan to be gone long.

He drove to a spot just past where the women had picnicked regularly last summer. Cole backed his pickup into an overgrown laneway on the far side of a Siberian elm, edged his seat to a flat position and settled in to wait. The women wouldn't be much longer at their partying.

His truck could probably be spotted if anyone were to look for him, but the women had no reason to. Or, if their headlights picked up the nose of his truck—every one of them knew his truck—inching out from behind the tree on their way out, they were free to guess the truth…that he liked to watch out for them.

To watch out for Honey.

She might not be the right partner for him, but he loved her, and his decision that he couldn't pursue her was his burden to bear.

Last summer, he'd sat out here on a number of Sunday nights watching until the women got in their vehicles to drive home, making sure they left the area safely.

He remembered thinking at the time that he should get a life, and that the townspeople could take care of themselves when he was off duty.

Well, he sure had a life this summer, didn't he?

Those children and the house would keep him busy.

Fifteen minutes later, a vehicle passed his truck, and another and another—all but Honey's.

She would be along soon.

He waited. And waited. And became worried.

It was taking too long.

Where was she?

Why hadn't she followed the other women out?

Had something happened to her?

He waited five more minutes. Dusk was falling. He pulled out and drove down the road to park on the shoulder just this side of the track leading to the stream.

He got out and walked down the track quietly—if someone had come along to hurt her, he needed the element of surprise.

In the clearing, he found a picnic blanket with glasses and two empty bottles of white wine, not enough for any of the women to have had too much to drink before driving home.

In the dying light of the sunset, the remnants of a small picnic dinner sat beside a bunch of clothes.

Now why would there be discarded clothing?

His gaze shot toward the water.

A body floated midstream.

Dear God. Honey!

Fully clothed, he dived into the lake and swam to the center, where the pale body was indeed Honey, eyes closed, body still.

He grabbed her to save her. She turned into a wildcat, fighting him. Not dead. Just floating.

"Honey!" he shouted. "It's Cole."

She stilled in his arms, staring with wide eyes. "What are you doing here? Why did you grab me?"

"I thought you were drowning." Now he could see clearly what he hadn't discerned from the shore. Honey had been enjoying a quiet, solitary skinny-dip in the lake. Naked.

"This isn't how drowning people look." She sounded cross, and breathless. "I would have been facedown, under the water."

He knew that. He had first aid training out the wazoo. "You were still. You were pale and...unmoving. I panicked."

"You scared me. I thought you were a stranger attacking me."

"You could have drowned, out here alone with no one the wiser."

"I wasn't drowning!" she shouted.

"You could have been. Or a snake could have swum into the water. Or a stranger could have found you, out here in the middle of nowhere alone and naked."

"You forgot about the rabid raccoons!" she yelled back.

"What raccoons?"

"The ones that don't exist! Just like the stranger who doesn't exist. I was not drowning. I was not in danger."

Her hands clung to his shoulders. Angry nails dug into his skin.

His hands encircled her waist, her soft, wet, unclothed skin cool to the touch in the still water of the lake warmed by the recent high temperatures.

His breath rattled out of him in sharp gusts.

Angry and scared, unable to speak, hands shaking beyond control, he grasped her face and kissed her, the language of his fear spoken with an invading tongue and mobile lips.

Chapter Twelve

Her response, fueled by anger, as unbridled as his, in-flamed his desire.

Cole lost his precious control, his reason, his measured mastered response to Honey.

He'd wanted her for an eternity, for ages before he had ever existed on this earth, his cells floating in the universe looking for a home.

Here. Honey. Home.

His mind had resisted Honey for years, but his heart had known.

He'd been a fool for ever trying to stop what had to happen.

She joined him fully, pulling his shirt out of his jeans and ripping open the buttons, undoing his buckle and un-zipping his jeans.

Crickets sang and a soft breeze hummed, the only music they needed to serenade them under the gathering stars.

Her body, slick with cooling water, ran like silk under his palms, full breasts with peaked nipples, a tiny waist and full hips—his idea of perfection, of womanhood.

Her generosity, apparent in every part of her life, flow-ered full-blown into passion and surrounded him.

Her arms slid around his neck, her palms holding his

head in place to deepen an already deep kiss, and her legs circled his waist, strong, her core seeking.

He entered her. Heaven had been here waiting for him all along.

Waist-deep water swirled around them. Cole's wet shoulders cooled in the night air while heat built below in moisture and passion.

Honey's tongue tasted of wine and chocolate and sweet, sinful longing.

Her hair, her arching back, her full behind…all were magnets that drew his big palms to explore.

To the rising rhythm of their lovemaking, water churned, exquisite fervor built and they came in joyful surrender.

Cole's love too massive for words or thought, he drank in Honey's sighs.

In the subsequent quiet, his pounding heart calmed and finally stilled. Against the cool skin of his chest, he felt Honey's heartbeat. It, too, calmed in time.

Her head lay against his shoulder as she rested boneless and sated in his arms, her trust humbling.

In his wildest dreams, he had never imagined it could be this…fulfilling, beautiful, incomparable.

He'd never experienced the rare spectacle of passion with not just desire but also love.

He trailed kisses across her shoulders. She shivered.

"Cold?" he murmured.

"Only my back. My wet hair." She sounded breathless.

He felt breathless.

She had robbed him of his sanity, his reasoned, controlled response to life.

He knew he should carry them to the blanket, but not yet. Not yet.

He cooled in the now-tranquil water.

Maybe this should be all of life, this peace and acceptance. This beauty in the darkness. This slice of outstanding respite from reality.

Maybe *this* should be reality.

Maybe tomorrow should take care of itself.

But that wasn't Cole's way. He knew better.

He knew how fleeting this was. His responsibilities were real and calling.

With regret, he carried Honey out of the water. He should put her down. He couldn't. He held on for just a few more moments, because tomorrow would come quickly enough. Too soon. And then he would be Sheriff Payette again and she would be a business owner, and this fantasy interlude would be over.

He lay down with her in his arms, brushed aside the detritus of the picnic and curled the two sides of the quilt over them.

"Warm enough?" he murmured.

"Hmm." She lay curled against him, this miracle of womanhood. "What was that about?" she asked, her breath fluttering across the bare skin of his chest.

Inside the cocoon of the blanket, he feathered his fingers down her spine, touching tiny knobs of delicate bone belying Honey's strength, both physical and of spirit.

She raised up on her hands to hover above him. Light from the rising moon, oblique across the water, lit her breasts, full on a tiny woman's frame.

She was perfect.

He'd sensed the danger in losing control.

Now he knew the peril of loving Honey intimately. How was he to take it back? How could he keep his distance when he'd tasted the beauty of Honey's lovemaking?

She was every bit as wild as he'd feared, out here alone naked in the water. An untamed nymph. A goddess.

Tension as dark and edgy as unwanted temptation knifed through him.

Before he could sink into Honey again, before he could indulge the man who wanted what could never be, he lifted her from him, rose and stalked away.

At the truck, he rummaged in the back until he found the bag of spare clothes he kept there.

WHAT ON EARTH just happened?

Cole had happened.

Honey lay on her back staring at the pinpricked night sky. Tiny hard dots of silver sparkled in the blue blackness of the night ceiling.

The breeze kicked up and cooled her damp skin.

She stood slowly, legs weak and shaky.

Boy, had Cole ever happened.

She'd been minding her own business when Cole Payette had swept her off her water-logged feet like a fire-breathing dragon, hot and angry.

His fierce lovemaking…

How was she to forget his lovemaking?

Where did they go from here?

Anywhere?

No. Not judging by the way he'd stomped off, angry with her.

She'd done nothing wrong.

Whatever was going on with Cole was his problem, not hers.

It did leave her with a new realization, though. She loved Cole. Good, decent, honorable, screwed-up Cole. It had snuck up on her when she wasn't looking.

She didn't want a cop, a deputy, a sheriff. She wanted safety and security…without the possibility of more heartache. She'd lost her father, her mother and Daniel. A heart could take only so much grief.

The impregnable walls she'd built against falling in love with the most unsuitable type of man had just crumbled.

Sighing, she dried off with the towel she'd packed for the evening and got dressed. Mere minutes later, she left the clearing as spotless as she'd found it.

She'd lost a battle. Now she needed to see if she'd lost the war.

At the end of the trail, she found her car boxed in by Cole's pickup truck. He stood beside his driver's door, big and silent and hard, in dry clothes.

Even from a distance she could sense his refusal to accept all that had just happened, the earth-shattering passion that had heated the water around them like magma rising from the earth.

She knew him well, could read him effortlessly. He'd gathered his defenses around himself.

It angered her. She wouldn't be used and thrown away.

But he hadn't used her. He'd loved her, his passion springing from fear. For her. She had participated fully. It was that simple.

Yes, she understood, but this push-pull that was Cole's desire for both love and control had to end.

Dropping her bag onto the ground, she came right up to him, grasped his face before he could object and took his mouth with her own.

He tried to push her away—oh, how he tried—but couldn't. He opened his mouth, thrust his tongue into hers and played a mighty tune.

She played right back.

When she finished, she said, "I know you, Cole. You're going to control the daylights out of this situation. Tomorrow morning, you're going to pretend this never happened."

His heavy breath ruffled strands of hair drying around her face.

She released him, stepped back and pointed her finger at him. "This isn't over."

"It is." He sounded like he'd been running uphill.

"Not by a long shot, buddy."

She stalked to her car and climbed in.

He stood like a Norse god, immobile. A wall of opposition.

She waited him out, refusing to tell him to move his vehicle.

Slowly, never moving his eyes from her shadowy presence in her car, he opened his door and climbed in, the vehicle shifting with his weight.

His headlights blinded her. She turned hers on and hoped she'd blinded him.

Dueling headlights.

He backed out and tore off down the highway.

Cole Payette was so far out of his trademark control that Honey laughed out loud.

She didn't know why.

If Cole didn't want her as she was, there wasn't a damned thing she could do about it.

Fine.

She could accept that. She would not ignore what had happened tonight, though.

She would remember making love in the water with Cole with the joy it deserved.

For, no doubt, many nights to come she would celebrate the memories.

To be honest with herself, she didn't know why she'd pushed Cole so hard. She was as lost as him. After all, she couldn't commit to him when he was sheriff any more than he would commit to her—and he would never give up his career.

She would never ask.

HONEY HEARD THAT Cole went back to work the next day.

She wondered how Maria was doing with the children, but she refused to walk over to the house to find out.

Cole and Maria had to work things out on their own.

She decided that she would, however, visit Cole after the children were in bed that evening. It was time for them to hash things out.

What they had done together couldn't be ignored. They had a lot of years left to live in this town. They had to find a way to get along.

She arrived at nine thirty, long after he should have the children settled, but early enough for him to still be up.

A lone lamp burned in the living room.

She knocked on Cole's front door softly.

When he opened the door, he took her breath away, solid and tempting. Images of last night's lovemaking flashed through her.

She thought they might have done the same to him, because his cheeks turned suspiciously pink.

"We need to talk."

"No, Honey, we really don't."

"Yes, Cole. Please."

He hung his head, sighed and opened the door wider. "Fine. Let's get this done."

She sidled past him and into the living room. She heard the front door close and Cole come up behind her. He gestured toward the sofa.

"Sit."

She did and started in without preamble.

"You love me." Baldly stated, but only bold talk would get them through this. "For some reason that escapes me, you don't want to love me."

When he would have answered, she raised one hand. "Let me finish, and then it will be your turn.

"I've come to realize that I care deeply for you, too,

but I can't. I won't let it happen because of what I went through when Daniel died. So here we are, two people who care for each other but have decided not to." She curled her legs up beside her and hugged a pillow to her chest. "And yet we have to live in the same town. How are we going to do that?"

He didn't respond.

"I suggest that we talk about our reasons for not wanting to pursue a relationship, so we can understand where the other is coming from."

Seated in an armchair across from her, he threw back his head and stared at the ceiling. When he finally straightened, he met her eye, expression tormented.

"I don't want to hurt you," he said.

"What could you possibly say to hurt me? That you love me but don't like me?"

"No, not exactly."

Meaning exactly. "You'd better explain, Cole, because nothing you can say will be worse than what I'm thinking. I'm not a horrible person, but you're about to give me a complex."

"No. You're a fantastic person, but…"

He leaned forward and rested his elbows on his knees. While staring at the floor, he told her about his life growing up in Georgia and then running away with a woman named Shiloh.

It all became clear.

"You think I'm as irresponsible as that woman."

"No. Maybe. Sort of. You're responsible at work, with your business, but the rest of the time, you have too much fun."

"There's such a thing?"

"Yes! You dance in the street. You put on those match-making nights that only invite trouble. You dance too close to the edge of the stream. You go skinny-dipping alone."

You dance too close to the edge of the stream. There was a powerful metaphor in there somewhere.

"Those are my moments of joy," Honey said. "I work hard. I need to let loose."

"But—"

"I'm not frivolous." She tossed the pillow aside. "How do you think I run the bar so well?"

"The bar, yes, but the rest…"

"I like to have fun. The deaths of my loved ones taught me that life is short and that I need to make my own joy."

"You do know how to do that." His admiration sounded grudging.

"You're so full of fear."

"Me? What about you?"

"What do you mean what about me?"

"Daniel."

One word, a name that filled her with so much pain.

"I'm not Daniel," he said. "Sure, I'm a lawman like he was, but I'm not young like him. I have experience. Plus, I'm smart. I don't try to stop speeding bullets or trains with my body."

Afraid to ask, nonetheless she put her question into words. She'd ignored a resolution to her loss for too long. "What happened that night, Cole? What *really* happened? You've never told me. You've always been careful to change the subject. Was Daniel's death his own fault?"

"I haven't wanted you to know."

She squeezed her eyes shut then opened them wide. "I need to hear the truth."

He sighed. "Yeah, I guess you do. Daniel was too new. He'd only been a deputy a month."

"I remember."

"When that guy came screaming through town in that stolen truck, Daniel shouldn't have gone after him alone.

He should have called for backup and waited to take him down, but he called and then took off after the guy."

"Daniel was keen. Too excited about the job. He wouldn't have waited."

Cole looked surprised.

"I knew him well, Cole."

"Yeah, you did." He tucked one fist inside the other. "Anyway, the guy crashed just outside town. Daniel got out of the squad car to make sure he hadn't killed himself. Another thing he shouldn't have done."

Honey nodded. "He should have waited in the car even if the guy was dying." Daniel's life or a criminal's life? No comparison. Pain cut through Honey's chest. Life was so unfair.

"But the guy wasn't dead," Cole said. "He reversed his truck and hit Daniel, pinning him against his squad car."

Cole stared at the floor between his feet. What wasn't he telling her?

"I know most of this," Honey said, "but I've always felt like there was more."

"There was."

When Cole hesitated, Honey asked, "Who found him?"

"Me." When he spoke again, his voice shook. "I wanted to call you so you could say goodbye."

Honey's spine stiffened. "But...but how? He died instantly."

"No. That's the story the sheriff wanted you to know. I was only a deputy back then and did as I was told. I lied to you, Honey. He was alive for a while."

"Then why didn't you call me? I would have come. I would have held him."

"He told me not to. He thought it would hurt you more to watch him die than to learn of his death later. He could barely talk, but that much he told me clearly enough."

Silent tears streamed down Honey's cheeks. *Daniel,*

you dear sweet fool. "I would have put up with the pain just to say goodbye."

"That's what I told him, but he was adamant. How could I go against a dying man's wishes?"

Honey bent forward and struggled to draw air into her lungs. A flash of anger shot through her. Cole should have called her. A reasoning voice brushed the anger aside. *No, he should have respected Daniel's wishes, Honey, exactly as he did.*

Minutes later, Honey pulled herself together. Cole had done the right thing. "I don't blame you, Cole."

He sighed, long and loud. "I thought you would."

"It was better to give a dying man what he wanted than to care about my feelings at that moment."

Cole made a noncommittal sound, perhaps not as convinced as she that he'd done the right thing.

Honey hadn't talked about Daniel in years. She felt the need now, with Cole. "Daniel was it, Cole. I was young, but I knew my own mind. I loved him."

"You seemed so together after his death. Everyone wanted to help, but you were kind of in this sturdy, independent world all to yourself."

"I had to be. I was barely hanging on, but I couldn't stand a repeat of what happened after my dad died."

"What happened then?"

"I was six. It was a heart attack. He was too young, but it happens."

She was silent for a while, remembering too many adults bending over her, petting her hair, kissing her cheek. She had just wanted to be alone with her mom, curled up in her lap. She had wanted her daddy back.

"Everyone was nice, but they felt sorry for me," she said. "They pitied me. All I heard everywhere I went was *poor Honey.* It was unbearable. I hated it."

She swiped at her cheeks. "I'd been robbed of so much,

and to top it off I was being robbed of my identity. Even as a little girl, I sensed it. For a long time afterward I was nothing but *that poor girl*, and I wouldn't let that happen again."

"So you handled Daniel's death alone. You suffered in silence."

"Yeah. Even with my mom I was strong."

"And then, a year later, your mom died."

"Yeah." Honey eased back into the sofa and wrapped her arms around herself.

After a thoughtful silence, she said, "Cole?"

"Hmm?"

"After my mom died, I really appreciated how you started coming around on the weekends and helping in the bar."

She picked at a loose thread on the arm of the sofa.

"I was capable and I had a good staff, but it was reassuring that this big solid guy was there in case I needed him. I've never thought until this moment how much that meant to me. I guess I kind of took you for granted."

"I wanted to do it."

Cole broke yet another long silence. "As long as I wear a uniform, you won't have anything to do with me, will you?"

"Your job can be dangerous. I can't lose another man I care about to a violent end."

Honey stood to leave but had to ask one last thing.

"Cole, what's wrong with us? We're both so afraid, yet we have a huge capacity for love. How do we get past our fears?"

"I don't know, Honey." He sighed and it sounded like he dredged it up from the soles of his feet. "I wish I did."

IT WAS THE last contact Honey had with Cole for a while. Over the next week, she didn't see him or the children much. Her life returned to normal.

She should have been grateful. Instead, she wandered her apartment at a loss. Her life didn't *feel* normal.

Too much had changed.

She hadn't even been able to dismantle the children's cave. The living room felt bare enough with them gone, without removing all traces of their presence.

Her entire week seemed to consist of crowds in the bar and an empty, lonely apartment.

The following Sunday, she rattled around with nothing to do.

Just when she most needed her sense of contentment, of having her life arranged exactly as she wanted it, her sense of well-being deserted her.

Lost, she phoned Rachel.

"Can I come over?" she asked when Rachel answered.

"Feeling lonely?" How like Rachel to *know*. How like her to hit the nail on the head on the first try.

A lie wouldn't work. She couldn't fool her best friend. "Yes," she admitted. There. She'd said aloud what she'd tried to deny to herself.

Loneliness swamped her.

She wanted to live with the children.

She wanted to share her bed with Cole.

At Rachel's house, she allowed the balm of Travis and Rachel's affection and Tori's enthusiasm for life wash over her.

For the first time, envy stirred in her.

She wanted what Travis and Rachel had, the love and tenderness, and the family.

She wanted children.

When Travis cleared the dinner table, he brushed his hand across Rachel's neck. Sure, their love was still new, but it went far beyond infatuation.

Probably twenty years from now Travis would still find

ways and opportunities to touch his wife…and Rachel would return his affection.

Cole Payette had interrupted what Honey had thought of as a good life.

He'd shattered her happiness. *No, be more accurate. Call it what it really was. Contentment.*

Her life hadn't been about happiness, no matter how hard she'd tried to find her joy wherever she could.

But since Cole had brought the children to town, to her apartment, and had made himself a part of her daily routine, he'd shattered her illusions.

She wanted more. She wanted *more*, dammit.

Their problems were twofold. His fear. Her fear.

What a pair of cowards.

OVER THE FOLLOWING two weeks, Honey saw them around town—Cole and the children in the diner, Cole in his uniform on his beat, Maria and the children walking down the street toward the playground.

Maddy even held Maria's hand when they crossed the street. Progress. Nice.

Cole's stool had sat empty in the bar for two weekends. Honey ached.

She missed them. She missed him.

One day, on her way into the diner for lunch, she passed Cole's parents coming out.

She'd seen them around town, of course, but never as closely as this. What had they found to do with themselves over the past three weeks?

Frank smiled at her.

Ada frowned.

She couldn't possibly be as cold as she looked, could she?

Cole thought so, and his opinion was good enough for Honey. He should know. He'd been raised by the woman.

Honey stood back to let them pass and said, "Hello. Lovely day."

Frank said, "Yes. Beautiful."

Ada said nothing.

They walked away down the street.

"Strange, cold people." Vy's voice behind Honey caught her attention.

"Why do you think they're staying in town?" Honey asked.

"Because she's still taking Cole to court. Apparently, tomorrow."

Honey's blood went cold. She hadn't heard. How could she not have? Why hadn't Cole shared that with her?

Because he'd been avoiding her.

Tomorrow. She would be there.

"With all of the hostility toward them in town," Vy started, "why come to the diner? They could eat at the restaurant in the next town."

Honey frowned. "Good question. And why have their lunch here? Has anyone talked to them?"

"Not really. Everyone's been decent. They don't get snubbed, but no one strikes up a conversation, either."

"So, again, why stay in town?"

"Know what I think?" Vy rested a hand on her hip.

"What?"

"They're keeping an eye on Cole."

"But he's no longer in my apartment. He's got a house and Maria Tripoli as a nanny. What on earth is wrong with any of that?"

"I don't know, Honey, but they spend a lot of time in one of the front booths staring at the cop shop across the street. Every so often, Frank takes out a little notebook and writes something."

A coldness that had nothing to do with the temperature ran through Honey.

Cole's parents were spying on him and the children. "What can they hope to find?" she asked.

"I think they want to prove that his job is dangerous and that he shouldn't be a parent or a guardian."

"For God's sake, that's ludicrous. He's smart. He's careful. He's mature. He takes precautions."

Honey stopped, stared at Vy and realized the full import of her words. She'd just repeated Cole's arguments for why he wasn't a risk as a lover.

If he was safe enough to be a guardian, surely he was safe enough to be a partner?

While she ate lunch, she sat in a window booth and watched the cop shop, thinking. Thinking about her own cowardice and willingness to let love escape because one of them might not live into old age.

Whey deny love because of fear? She was a fool.

She watched Cole come and go about his usual sheriff's business. Today, that business looked innocuous, except for the effect just seeing Cole had on Honey.

Good thing he wasn't here beside her, or she would have trouble not touching him.

When Vy brought her bill, she said, "I'm scared. What have they got on Cole that they can use against him?"

"I don't know, Honey. I wish I did."

Honey left the diner and marched to her bar.

Once inside, she found Chet in the kitchen.

"If I double tomorrow afternoon's staff, can you cover for me while I go to Cole's court date? For all I know, it could take all day tomorrow."

"Of course. You can leave early tonight and sleep in."

On impulse, she hugged him. "You're the best, Chet. Thanks."

Honey did leave the bar early that night to go to bed at a good time, but she hardly slept.

She got up early and dressed with care.

She tried to eat breakfast, but nerves fluttered through her stomach. Halfway through her bowl of cereal, she gave up. Her tummy wasn't going to take any more.

She had a plan.

Cole would kill her, but it needed to be done.

She'd come to realize she'd do just about anything to make sure those children stayed with him where they belonged.

Chapter Thirteen

Two hours later, Honey sat in a courtroom with many of her friends and townspeople from Rodeo. With no small separate family court available, they'd all settled into the largest courtroom in the county.

The judge heard a statement from Ada, all of it the kind of stuff Honey expected—about their wealth, their position in their hometown, their ability to send the children to the best schools and blah, blah, blah.

When she started in on Cole's job, Honey's heart filled with icy rage.

"My son is a violent man, Your Honor. He could have had a good career as a lawyer, but instead he is punching people and throwing them across barrooms."

She went on to describe the incident with the stranger who had nearly raped Honey.

Her interpretation—that Honey had welcomed the man's advances, that Cole had caught them making out and had been jealous and consequently behaved violently—sent spears of anger flaring through Honey. Panic followed that. What if the judge believed the woman?

Honey's optimism sank to the soles of her shoes.

They had money. They had prestige. They had standing in their town.

And they were bad-mouthing Cole, the best man on the face of the earth.

Cole had standing in his community, too, but did it compare? Could he compete?

Honey just didn't know.

When Ada finished speaking and it looked like the judge was taking her seriously, Honey panicked.

No.

Cole couldn't possibly lose those children.

It would break his heart.

While the judge read papers in front of him, Honey made up her mind. This called for desperate measures.

"Your Honor," she blurted before she even knew she was going to open her mouth.

He glanced up, eyebrows raised.

"Who just spoke?"

Never in her life had Honey been timid, but worry for Cole, and fear that she might make a mistake, turned her weak.

She stood and raised her hand.

"I did, Your Honor."

Desperate times. Desperate measures.

The judge cut her with a laser glare. "You can't just speak out in court without permission."

"Your Honor, may I have permission?"

The judge stared at Honey for so long she started to squirm. She wasn't a squirmer by nature, but what she was about to do would take every scrap of courage she had.

"Why?" he asked.

"Because I'm Honey Armstrong, the woman about whom Mrs. Payette was telling lies."

"The woman from the bar incident?"

Honey shivered. "It was far more than an incident, Your Honor."

"Okay, step forward and stand there beside Sheriff Payette. Tell me what happened."

She did, in detail, including outlining her terror.

When she finished, the judge considered what she'd said. He took too long.

"There's one more thing, Your Honor."

COLE STARED DOWN at Honey. What on earth was she doing? It was great that she'd set the record straight on that night, but what else was there that she could add?

"This is highly irregular," the judge said. "Whatever else you have to say— Okay, how germane is it to the case?"

"It's essential that you hear this one last thing."

Honey shifted beside Cole. She refused to meet his eye, he noted.

What mischief was she up to?

"Go ahead," the judge ordered. "Speak."

Honey twisted her fingers together. Odd to see her nervous when she could handle just about anything.

"I noticed that Mrs. Payette, in her petition, left out one very important point. A *crucial* point, Your Honor. She stated that Cole shouldn't be allowed to raise the children because he's a single guy. First, that's hogwash. There are so many different forms of parenting these days that are successful. The old pattern of a father and a mother no longer has to exist. Single parents can do an amazing job, too."

The judge waited patiently, so Honey went on. "Cole's a good, decent, smart guy. He can raise those children on his own with one hand tied behind his back."

She wasn't sounding as articulate as usual, though her words warmed his heart. Her hands, he noted— when she wasn't twisting them together—shook. She was nervous.

So was he. A lot rode on the results of today's hearing. Cole had testified before in front of Judge Bailey and had always found the man enigmatic and unpredictable. "Secondly," she said, "he won't be single much longer. What Mrs. Payette failed to mention, perhaps because her *spying* on Cole hasn't uncovered it, is that Cole and I are engaged."

What? Once Cole started coughing, he couldn't stop. What the *hell* was she talking about? Yet again, Honey's impulses overrode common sense.

Fingering the sealed letter in his hand, he hoped it was a secret weapon he could use to win this case without Honey's well-meaning interference.

"Honey," he said, taking her firmly by the elbow. "This isn't necessary."

She rounded on him. "Oh, yes, it is, Cole. You should have shared our plans with Frank and Ada. Maybe then they wouldn't have thought to take you to court. They wouldn't have thought they could be successful."

"Your Honor, Ms. Armstrong has been premature with her pronouncement."

"You mean you *aren't* engaged?" A frown developed between the judge's formidable eyebrows.

Cole froze.

He couldn't call Honey a liar.

"Please, Cole," she whispered beside him. "I'm terrified for you and the children."

Her concern warmed him. Her heart was in the right place.

"Honey and I," he said carefully to evaluate the judge's response, "have an understanding."

The frown eased.

His bachelorhood wasn't a detriment to raising the children, but he'd worried anyway even though he was young with a secure future and a strong standing in the community. Despite it all, had Honey just saved the day? His mother had dressed as the wealthy high-society matron she was. She had pulled out all of the stops in her statement. Her lawyer stood beside her in expensive sartorial splendor. The judge understood exactly how healthy her resources were. She'd made him aware of the extent of her wealth.

By contrast, Cole had decided to represent himself. He'd spoken in court often enough.

He had a steady job and a lot of love, more information about the guy who'd attacked Honey, not to mention a letter from his sister that he'd never read.

Was it enough?

Cole, a man who never made snap decisions, made one now.

"We are engaged, yes. We were just waiting until the end of the summer, until after the work on the fair has settled down."

The judge hummed and nodded.

At the defendant's table, Cole and Honey stood side by side but worlds apart as the judge said, "Sheriff Payette, you said you had evidence to present?"

Finally. Why had he waited so long to ask for it?

"First, Your Honor, I'd like to add an update about the criminal who tried to rape Honey. He confessed that he'd been hired by my parents to harass her, perhaps with the purpose of scaring her so she would remove her support for me."

His mother gasped. Furious whispering erupted between her and his father. Rumblings ran through the spectators.

Cole thought he heard his father say, "I told you so."

"The prisoner has been found guilty," Cole continued. "He's awaiting sentencing."

"Is this true?" the judge asked of the Payettes.

"How could you—" Ada started, but Frank grasped her arm to cut her off.

"Yes, Your Honor, but he was never supposed to become violent."

Frank turned to Honey and said, "I deeply regret his actions and ours."

Cole stared at this stronger version of his father, and finally saw a glimpse of who the man might have been without Ada.

They'd just suffered a setback, but there was more.

"I have a letter from my sister, Your Honor, left with her lawyer and the will, to be used if my parents sued for custody."

"What does it say?" the judge asked.

"I don't know. It's sealed."

Cole handed the letter to the bailiff to pass along to the judge.

The judge acknowledged that the envelope was sealed. He opened it and read the letter.

When he finished, he appraised Cole and stared down Ada and Frank.

"This ought to be read aloud." He did just that.

To whom it may concern,

If you are reading this letter, I'm assuming you are a lawyer or a judge and my brother and the children are in trouble.

For years, my brother was the most important person in my life. He gave me comfort and love when they were missing from my parents.

He protected his baby sister from the day of my birth. When I cried, he held me. When I hurt, he soothed me. When I needed his help to leave a loveless home, he sent me money.

After my marriage, my husband took over Cole's protective role. We have two beautiful children.

If you are reading this, I am deceased and so is

my husband. I, and my husband, have left the care of our children to Cole.

For all intents and purposes, he raised me, not my parents. Cole is the kind of man I want to parent my children if Dennis and I aren't here.

I know my parents well. They will try to take Evan and Madeline in any way that they can, using any means. They will throw their money around. Cole does not have the same resources.

So I am here today, present in this letter, to say, don't. Do not, under any circumstances, give the care of my children to my parents.

They failed to offer a loving home to Cole and me as we grew up. I don't know how Cole turned out to be as strong and kind as he is. It must be strength of character and backbone, because he sure knew how to make me feel loved and protected in a house without love.

Leave my children with Cole and they will grow up to be as wonderful as he is.

All my love to my children and to my brother.
Alexandra Payette Engel

Cole held on by a thread, shaking with the force of the emotions coursing through him.

Sandy.

His sister's love for him took his breath away.

He wanted her here.

A letter was a poor substitute.

If he had her with him, he would hold her and never let go so nothing bad would happen to her.

But he had let her go, and she had married a good man and the two of them had died together, because of a moment of inattention or exhaustion, a deer running across a slippery road and a swerve into a tree.

He wiped his eyes.

He didn't care if his mother thought his tears a weakness. He didn't care if she saw them as a point of vulnerability she could use.

Sandy.

Aw, Sandy, come back.

Honey reached for his hand and held on.

The judge cleared his throat.

"Well. I guess that says it all, doesn't it? Mr. and Mrs. Payette, I see nothing to warrant the removal of the children from their uncle's care into yours.

"Your daughter loved him. She was of sound mind. She feared that you would bring this kind of action against your son, with good reason. We're here today because you didn't respect your daughter's wishes. I'm not sure I understand why.

"You have resorted to underhanded techniques to scare these people and to try to win your case. You have tried to make the sheriff appear unsafe for the children merely because of his profession.

"Sir and Madam, many people in dangerous professions enjoy long lives and successful marriages and meet their parental responsibilities.

"This court has seen Cole Payette's bank records and his pay stubs and has reviewed his work record. His sister confessed her deep love for him. She professed her trust in his ability to love the children. This court deems him eminently capable of raising them."

Ada gasped.

"Besides," the judge went on, a twinkle in his eye, "he's about to get married. This court rules in his favor."

His mother emitted a cry of outrage. She surged to her feet and then swayed.

"No. That's not possible."

"Ma'am, you will sit down and behave with decorum or I will find you guilty of contempt."

The judge folded the letter and sent it back to Cole. "My advice to you, Mrs. Payette, is to abide by your daughter's wishes, and mine, and let this issue rest. Don't pursue this in the future. Don't take it to a higher court. I guarantee you will lose."

Cole left the courtroom walking on a cloud.

It was done.

He could breathe again. Since the day his parents had come to town, his old neuroses had suffocated him.

They fell from him like water from the top of a cliff, a waterfall of fears and regrets cascading away.

When Sandy and Dennis died, he'd been afraid of the burden. Today, all he knew was joy.

The children were his.

Ada stormed past without a glance in his direction. His father walked by, nodded and offered a tentative smile.

Free at last of their influence, Cole's life would be perfect except for one pesky detail.

Honey Armstrong had declared in court in front of their friends and townspeople that they were getting married.

What was a man to do when all of his dreams were about to come true, but for all of the wrong reasons?

Chapter Fourteen

"Not one word."

That brief sentence spoken by Cole so harshly cut off Honey's explanation and silenced her effectively.

A slab of granite looked soft compared to Cole's jaw.

He must have understood her panic.

He must have felt it himself after his mother spoke, with her money and powerful clothing and her persuasion...and her unfair accusations!

But then there had been that revelation about the attacker and the letter.

It would have been enough.

So why hadn't Cole told her about it?

Because she should have trusted him, should have had faith that he was smart enough to convince the judge one way or another to grant him custody.

And Honey had ruined it. Maybe Cole was right. Maybe she was too impulsive, but in that courtroom, she had known real terror.

But what was the problem, really? The buzz would go around that they were engaged, they would say that they had changed their minds, and life would go on.

Except that she didn't want life to go on, not the way it had been. Not any longer.

In that courtroom, she had seen endless days stretching into eternity for Cole alone with the children.

And she had seen her life stretching into loneliness without either the children or Cole. How much was her fear worth? Why did she hold on to it so tenaciously?

With Cole in her future, there might come the phone call that every loved one of a lawman feared, the one she'd endured when she'd loved Daniel... Or it might never come.

They could live into ripe old age together.

Cole was strong and smart, a hell of lot less likely to go off half-cocked than Daniel had been.

They arrived at his house, and Honey hugged the children.

Maria went home and Cole sat the children down.

"You're going to stay with me. The judge said so."

"For real?" Evan shouted. "For ever and ever?"

"Yes. You are never going away from me, ever."

Madeline burst into tears. Honey understood why. She wanted to cry, too, overwhelmed by strong emotions.

Cole settled Madeline on his lap and soothed her while Evan whooped and raced around the living room. He took off his shoes and sock-skated down the hallway.

Honey felt the weight of her interference and intrusion into Cole's life. Sure, when he'd first arrived in town with the children, he'd asked for her help, but he had never asked for her to do so much, to go so far as to lie in court.

"I'd better go."

Madeline wriggled out of Cole's arms and rushed to Honey, throwing her arms around her.

Honey picked her up. "Are you happy?"

Maddy smiled, but her lower lip wobbled.

"Sometimes it feels too strong, doesn't it?"

Maddy nodded.

"Sometimes happiness hurts as much as sadness, but it's always better. Okay?"

Maddy nodded again.

"You will have a wonderful, absolutely fabuloso life with your amazing uncle Cole. Okay?"

Maddy said, "I love Uncle Cole."

She heard him clear his throat before saying, "Don't go, Honey. Stay for supper."

She watched him over Maddy's head and asked, "Are you sure?"

She really wanted to ask, *Why?*

She couldn't resist temptation. She wanted to stay and to spend time with three people who had become more important to her than anyone else in her life.

In a perfect world, she would live here with them. After dinner she would help ready the children for bed and then she would take their strong, wonderful uncle into her arms and love him silly.

Supper was a noisy affair because of Evan, who didn't sense the tension between Honey and his uncle.

As hard as Honey tried to keep a smile on her face, she thought Madeline might have known.

Cole asked her to help get the children ready for bed, just as she had imagined doing, and it was so bittersweet she nearly came undone.

She wouldn't be able to do this again. While it felt like heaven to her, it was also too painful.

After the children went to bed, she and Cole went downstairs.

They finished the dishes, and then he stalked to the living room, where he stood staring out the front window, back rigid.

"Don't shut me out, Cole. Talk to me."

He didn't respond.

"Rant at me if you want to."

Still, he kept his own counsel, but glared at her over his shoulder.

Enough, already. Her remorse morphed into anger.

"Yes, I was impulsive today. I tried to control what went on in that courtroom. My employees classify me as a benevolent dictator."

Cole didn't smile.

"You can be angry with me as much as you like, but I was terrified. And it's not the end of the world. For God's sake, we'll tell the town that we've decided we don't suit and we'll call it off."

"We can't."

Honey frowned. "Why not?"

"The children will hear about it through the grapevine."

"The children," she breathed and covered her mouth with her hand. In trying to save them, she would end up hurting them.

"Those kids would like nothing more than for you and me to be together, to be married and raising them as a family. You know that, don't you?"

"You're right. I didn't think ahead."

"You never do." He sounded bitter.

Anger curdled Honey's blood. "Okay, stop right there. I have my faults, but you don't get to stand there and pretend that you're perfect."

Cole glared at her. "This I've got to hear. What's wrong with me?"

"You're a controller. You control your deputies and everyone around you. You control this entire town, for that matter, Sheriff."

"So what? I'm tasked with keeping law and order."

"It spills over into the rest of your life. Sometimes it's your way or the highway. Today I took a tiny bit of control away from you in that courtroom and you're freaking out."

Cole's brow furrowed and he thought. In his deep, quiet way, Cole thought some more. And more.

His shoulders slumped.

"God, you're right."

He collapsed into an armchair and breathed heavily into his hands.

"Cole, don't beat yourself up. You're not saying anything, but I can see you doing it. It's written all over your face. That wasn't my intention. I just need you to see that my flaws are not gigantic and they aren't unreasonable. Everyone has them. Even you."

"This is bad, though." He dropped his hands. He looked like she'd punched him. "Honey, sit. Please. I have things I need to tell you."

At the regret and sorrow on his face, her anger dissipated. She sat on the sofa opposite him.

"You saw my mother. You've met my father. You know the dynamic there."

She made a sound to indicate she wanted to know more.

"You know what's appalling about what you said? It's true. I tried so hard to walk away from the very thing I've been doing. You're right. I need to be sheriff. I need to control. I need the town to be safe."

"But see, Cole, I don't want you beating yourself up, because what you exercise in town is a different kind of dominance than you experienced in your childhood. There isn't a person in this town—other than me just now, because I needed to defend myself—who thinks that what you do is wrong. They are happy that you keep the peace, and law and order, and make them feel safe.

"For that, the town is eternally grateful."

COLE LOATHED, ABSOLUTELY abhorred what Honey said about him, even if it was true.

Lord, *because* it was true.

He'd traveled so far, both physically and metaphorically,

to get away from his upbringing, only to find he was every bit as controlling as his mother and grandmother.

One thought shot horror through him.

"What about the children? How do I protect them from me?"

"Cole, there's nothing to protect them from. You need to understand the varying, subtle degrees of control. Yes, even control can be subtle. You don't dominate. Trust me. Those children will thrive under your care and leadership. You will guide them, not dominate them as your family did with you."

He stared as though seeing a new side of Honey. "How did you get to be so wise?"

"Believe it or not, I've lived through a lot. My dad died when I was six. Daniel died when I was twenty-one. Mom died when I was twenty-two. I'm alone now. I need to accept that and be strong."

Cole's pulse started up a staccato beat because of what he was about to do. Did he have the courage?

"No," he said.

"No?"

Heart in his throat, Cole approached and lifted her to her feet. He cradled her head with his palm and brushed her cheek with his thumb. "You aren't alone."

"But...what do you mean?"

He'd been forced into a false engagement. Now that it existed, did he really want it to end? He desired Honey every bit as much as he ever had—maybe more since making love to her that one perfect night.

His dream was coming true.

She watched him, intelligence shining in the depths of her beautiful eyes, and he wondered why he hadn't, in the years he'd known her, honored her backbone and her strong sense of responsibility.

He'd allowed his experience growing up, and Shiloh's betrayal, to rule his actions and his thoughts.

Honey could be controlling, when she had to be, and joyful, when she needed it. She balanced one with the other.

Only in his own mind did he think she went too far.

If he looked at her through the eyes of a healthy, courageous man, without fear, he saw her in all of her strength and glory.

His thumb feathered across her lips. She closed her eyes.

"No," he whispered.

Mesmerized, she asked, "No? What was the question?"

Cole smiled. He liked that she was so deeply affected by his touch.

"No, you aren't alone."

What he wanted most in the world was to order Honey to stay with him, to forbid her to ever leave.

Cole Payette wanted Honey Armstrong for the rest of his life.

Of course, it was her choice. And he would honor Honey's choices, and her freedom, and her backbone from now on.

"Do you want to end our engagement?" he asked and held his breath. The wrong answer would hurt. It would come close to destroying him. He would curse every single day he lived in the same town as Honey and couldn't touch her, couldn't breathe in her unique scent and make love to her.

"The bigger question, Cole, is do *you*? You know who I am. You know the parts of my character that you don't like."

"And I know the parts I do. I like these." He feathered a touch over her lips again. His palm circled her neck. His fingers caressed her nape. "I like this." His hand stroked her hair, from top to bottom, whispering along her spine on the way. "I love this."

Up at her neck, he edged her blouse off one shoulder. One finger ran across her collarbone. "I really like clavicles."

"Clavicles?"

"Uh-huh. Yours are wonderful."

"They are?"

His fingers cupped her bare shoulder, her soft skin almost bringing him to the brink of action.

"I like your strong shoulders." His fingers curled around to her back.

"My shoulders?"

With both hands, he held her upper back and drew her close. When her chest touched his, he said, "And I like those."

"Those?" She seemed to have become incoherent, capable only of repeating what he said.

Cole liked it. He liked her losing her train of thought. He liked her succumbing to temptation. To *his* temptation.

"Those absolutely gorgeous, perfect breasts. I want them in my hands, Honey. Bare and peaking."

Eyes closed, she swayed forward before catching herself. Her eyelids popped open.

She shook herself and seemed to come out of a trance. She put distance between them. "Physical attraction won't last forever," she said briskly. For a moment she had succumbed to his caresses and he'd liked her capitulation, but it was too brief. "We need more."

"Do you think, after fourteen years in this town, all I feel for you is physical attraction? Do you think I love only your body? Don't you know how much I admire you? How much of your character I find perfect?"

He held her arms. "Do you honestly think I find your body more attractive than your decency and honesty? Do you think I don't admire what a good businesswoman you are? Do you think I don't appreciate your energy, and your smiles and generosity, and your willingness to help your neighbors, and above all your loving character?"

Her cheeks had pinked with his lengthy description, but she stayed close.

"And all of my crazy talk about your fun-loving nature being wrong was exactly that. Crazy. The problem was me, not you. I need your fun, Honey. I need you to help me to lighten up. I need your joy."

A smile like a slow-rising dawn spread across her face.

"I like that, Cole."

He returned her smile, at peace at last, his demons exorcised, his dragons slayed.

Escaping his mother's extreme control, he'd then given his life over to Shiloh. But Honey didn't ask for control. She asked for an equal share. That he could do.

"Cole, I love all of this talk about character, but now I find—I want— The children are asleep and we're two adults alone and attracted to each other."

His thumb had migrated to her throat. He felt her swallow. He felt her pulse pound.

"I mean, *really* attracted," she said. "Can we go up to your bed?"

"That's exactly where I want you." When she moved toward the stairs, he stopped her and held her by her waist so she wouldn't go farther.

"First, we have to settle about my job."

"I see you differently. I see you as a lover and a loved one and as a future partner. I can't think of anyone I want more in my life and beside me for the rest of my days than you."

He held her and sighed. Maybe all of his impossible, crazy dreams were about to come true.

"I love you, Cole. I want to truly be engaged to you. I want to lay down all of my fears and never give them another moment's consideration..."

His arms held her as close as he could without hurting her, the depth of his love so powerful it could crush her.

"I want to marry you, Cole. I love you." She eased away to look into his face.

"I love you, too. I want you in my life, for all time."

A luminous smile turned his lovely lady into the prettiest woman in the universe.

"Speaking of desire…" she said, giggled and ran for the stairs.

He followed with long strides, picked her up in his arms and took the stairs two at a time.

In his bedroom, he dropped her onto his king-size bed. It was large enough, but missing something…

"We need to bring your bed here. We need to make love in it every night for the next fifty years."

"At least once a night." She grinned impishly.

He returned her grin. "At least once a night."

He locked the bedroom door, came back to Honey and slowly removed her clothing, paying homage to all of her interesting parts.

Much later, she paid homage to all of his.

IN THE MORNING, Honey sat at the breakfast table with Cole, Evan and Madeline.

She had wanted to go home in the early morning before the children got up, but Cole had resisted.

Now, he spoke up, the deep frown lines that had developed in the past few years eased with happiness. "Children, how would you feel about Honey coming to live with us?"

Evan shouted, "Yeah!"

Madeline's blue eyes, already too big for her tiny face, got even bigger.

She jumped down from her chair and scrambled into Honey's lap. "Yeah," she said, voice small but crystal clear.

"Is she gonna share Madeline's bedroom?" Evan asked.

"Nope," Cole said. "We're getting married. Honey's going to stay in my room."

Evan danced around the kitchen.

Madeline's chin wobbled. One tear slid down her cheek. Baffled and bewildered, Honey looked to Cole for help.

He didn't seem to know any more than she did. He took Maddy into his arms and held her tightly against his big, safe chest.

"Don't you want Honey to live here?" he asked.

She nodded.

"Don't you want her to share my room?"

She nodded again.

"Then what's wrong, sweetheart? Why are you crying?"

"Don't know."

"Oh, Cole," Honey said. "She's overwhelmed. All of these emotions are so huge."

She knelt on the floor in front of Madeline, between Cole's outstretched legs. "Are you too happy again?"

Maddy nodded.

Honey brushed her hair from her forehead. "It's a lot to take in, isn't it?"

Maddy nodded again. "You miss your mommy and daddy, don't you?"

Again the child nodded.

"I understand. You can tell me about them anytime you want to, okay?"

"Me, too?" Evan asked.

Honey wrapped an arm around him. Cole rested his hand on his hair.

"Yes, anytime."

Evan leaned his head on her shoulder.

"Can I do anything for you?" Honey asked Maddy.

"Want Tori."

"She always makes you feel better, doesn't she?"

"Yeah."

"Okay. I'll call Rachel. How about if you finish your breakfast while I call?"

Cole said, "Everything will be fine, Madeline and Evan. I guarantee it."

He put her on her own chair, and she picked up her spoon to eat her cereal. He directed Evan back to his own breakfast.

Honey called Rachel. Maybe what the children needed was a morning of uncomplicated fun.

After sharing her good news while Rachel whooped and simply *had* to share the news with Travis *immediately*, Honey asked, "Can you give Evan and Madeline a ride on the carousel?"

"Yes! Of course. Meet you there! I am *so* happy for you." Rachel hung up the phone, still laughing.

Honey felt the same way. She'd had a silly, sloppy grin on her face since she'd awakened. Maybe even before. Maybe she'd slept with a grin all night long.

Except when they'd made love.

Then she'd been oh so gloriously serious in her loving of Cole.

Back in the kitchen, she told the children they were going out to play somewhere special.

Cole raised a questioning eyebrow.

"I'm going home to change. I'll be back in half an hour."

"Where are we going after that?"

With a quick glance at the children, she said, "It's a surprise."

Evan perked up. "I like surprises!"

"Me, too," Maddy said, her voice getting stronger every day. Honey no longer had to lean close to hear her soft, restrained whispers. "Where's Tori?"

"You'll see her soon," Honey said before stepping out of the house.

She drove home, changed and washed up, and returned in record time.

Cole and the children waited for her on the front veranda, Evan hopping from foot to foot and Madeline in her favorite spot—the safest spot on earth for her—in Cole's arms with her head resting against his broad chest.

When Honey got out of her car and approached, he brushed his cheek on Maddy's hair and said something. She giggled. Actually giggled. Madeline spread her palm flat against his chest and said, "Again."

Whatever he had said, he repeated it and Maddy giggled again. "Rumbly!"

Cole laughed and Maddy's head followed the movement of his chest.

Honey's eyes watered.

Oh, great balls of freaking fire! At some point in the near future these spikes of emotion were going to have to stop or she would never survive.

"Come on," she said. "Let's get into Cole's truck."

Once they'd all loaded into the truck, Cole turned to her. "Where to?"

"The amusement park. Rachel's meeting us there."

"And Tori?" a tiny voice asked from the backseat.

"Yes, Tori will be there."

"'Kay."

Cole backed out of the driveway and drove to the park. He pulled up on the side of the road, and everyone got out.

Evan ran to the fence and stared openmouthed at the rides. "Wow."

When Cole lifted Madeline out of her car seat, she stared, too. In particular, the carousel—front and center—riveted her interest.

For all of last summer and well into the fall, Rachel had

scrubbed everything down, chipped away at old paint, applied new paint and fixed the engine.

The now-glistening carousel ride captured everyone's attention as they drove by.

The sign over the entrance had been scraped free of rust and verdigris and shone, as well.

Rodeo Amusement Park and Fair.

In less than a month, this old space would ring anew with workers and attendees.

Rachel hailed them from the center of the carousel.

Travis walked up with baby Beth in his arms and shook Cole's hand.

Tori ran over. "Sheriff, you gots to put Maddy down so I can hug her."

Cole laughed and deposited Maddy next to her friend.

After hugging, the children ran onto the carousel. "Evan, you come, too," Tori ordered. "We gots to choose our animals. Mommy is giving us a ride."

"Yeah!" Evan ran circles around the ride while Tori and Madeline walked more slowly, touching each animal and discussing its merits.

When the first owner had carved them, he'd chosen the most unusual animals to showcase. Along with the expected horses, they included local animals—a pair of bighorn sheep, a bison, a white-tailed deer, an elk and a huge bull, all wearing ornate saddles.

The children stopped and stared at a white horse with a pink, blue and gold saddle.

Madeline kept walking until she found a small pony. Shorter than the horse Tori had chosen, he was pink with a pure white saddle trimmed in gold.

She reached up and patted his nose.

Honey stepped up onto the ride. "Is that the one?"

Madeline smiled up at Honey. That smile, filled with

apprehensive joy, as though the child were afraid to be happy, melted Honey's heart.

In time, she vowed the joy would grow and the apprehension would fade.

COLE HELPED EVAN up onto the bull and placed his hand on his back.

Evan shrugged it off. "No, Uncle Cole. I can do it by myself. I'm big now."

Cole stood back and held onto a pole when the ride started, his hand hovering behind Evan's back in case it was needed.

The ride picked up speed. A calliope sounded in the background, a carnival version of the Beatles' "All You Need Is Love."

True. So insanely true.

He glanced to the little pony that Madeline rode. Honey had one hand on the child's shoulder.

Honey. His future wife.

His pleasure and joy.

Madeline squealed and laughed.

Talk about joy.

Cole had never heard anything so beautiful in his life.

The lessons overwhelmed him, but in the best way. Opening himself up to Honey and the children left him vulnerable, but what a small price to pay for this, here, now.

For a full life.

He thought his eyes might be tearing but blamed it on the wind.

When the ride slowed down and they all got off, Cole took Evan's hand and wrapped his other arm around Honey, who held a happily smiling Madeline.

He thought back to the devastation Sandy and Dennis's

deaths had wrought. He remembered walking into Honey's Place feeling helpless and alone and overwhelmed.

He'd wanted Honey's help.

He'd wanted Honey.

He'd certainly gone to the right place, hadn't he?

In a few short weeks, Cole had been transformed from lonely bachelor and sedate, practical town sheriff to the happiest family man on the face of the planet.

All you need is love.

Yes, indeed.

* * * * *

Be sure to pick up the earlier books in
Mary Sullivan's RODEO, MONTANA *miniseries:*
RODEO FATHER,
RODEO RANCHER and
RODEO BABY!
And look for Nadine's story, available in May 2018
from Harlequin Western Romance.

Get 2 Free Books,
Plus 2 Free Gifts—
just for trying the Reader Service!

♦ HARLEQUIN®
SPECIAL EDITION

HSE17R3

HOME on the RANCH

YES! Please send me the **Home on the Ranch Collection** in Larger Print. This collection begins with 3 FREE books and 2 FREE gifts in the first shipment. Along with my 3 free books, I'll also get the next 4 books from the Home on the Ranch Collection, in LARGER PRINT, which I may either return and owe nothing, or keep for the low price of $5.24 U.S./ $5.89 CDN each plus $2.99 for shipping and handling per shipment*. If I decide to continue, about once a month for 8 months I will get 6 or 7 more books, but will only need to pay for 4. That means 2 or 3 books in every shipment will be FREE! If I decide to keep the entire collection, I'll have paid for only 32 books because 19 books are FREE! I understand that accepting the 3 free books and gifts places me under no obligation to buy anything. I can always return a shipment and cancel at any time. My free books and gifts are mine to keep no matter what I decide.

268 HCN 3760 468 HCN 3760

Name   (PLEASE PRINT)

Address   Apt. #

City   State/Prov.   Zip/Postal Code

Signature (if under 18, a parent or guardian must sign)

Mail to the **Reader Service**:

IN U.S.A.: P.O. Box 1867, Buffalo, NY. 14240-1867
IN CANADA: P.O. Box 609, Fort Erie, Ontario L2A 5X3

* Terms and prices subject to change without notice. Prices do not include applicable taxes. Sales tax applicable in NY. Canadian residents will be charged applicable taxes. This offer is limited to one order per household. All orders subject to approval. Credit or debit balances in a customer's account(s) may be offset by any other outstanding balance owed by or to the customer. Please allow 3 to 4 weeks for delivery. Offer available while quantities last. Offer not available to Quebec residents.

Your Privacy—The Reader Service is committed to protecting your privacy. Our Privacy Policy is available online at www.ReaderService.com or upon request from the Reader Service.

We make a portion of our mailing list available to reputable third parties that offer products we believe may interest you. If you prefer that we not exchange your name with third parties, or if you wish to clarify or modify your communication preferences, please visit us at www.ReaderService.com/consumerschoice or write to us at Reader Service Preference Service, P.O. Box 9062, Buffalo, NY. 14240-9062. Include your complete name and address.

Get 2 Free Books,
Plus 2 Free Gifts—
just for trying the Reader Service!

◆HARLEQUIN *Desire*